To

Sim

I h

my first book

from a big fella

Steve

Because Anything you can do — we can do better!

MERCURY RAPIDS

Published in digital format by *Bookbooters.com*, 2002
First paperback edition published by *Bookbooters Press*, an imprint of *Bookbooters.com*, 2002

For information contact:
Bookbooters.com
14 Tomstead Road East
Simsbury, CT 06070-2006

http://www.bookbooters.com

ISBN: 1-59281-016-0

For Aiden...

PROLOGUE

The stars of the Milky Way burned fiercely in the permanent night of space. Although only tiny pinpoints of light, each of these stars was a sun in its own right, many with planets and, naturally, life.

Suddenly, the vista of stars distorted, their light coalescing and falling in on themselves, like water running down a plughole. From the centre of this vortex emerged a perfect equilateral triangle. The vast polygonal spacecraft would have been as black as the void itself were it not for the four evenly spaced lights that nestled on its belly, as brilliant as the vast furnaces beyond.

As the inky starship glided overhead, the deep space monitoring cameras on satellite 'M/OC47' followed its flight path with inhuman precision.

Out of the blackness appeared the immense curve of a blue-green world, the birthplace of the ever-vigilant satellite. 'M/OC47' watched impassively as the sleek, ebony craft plunged downwards into the atmosphere, its perfectly constructed hull causing no friction and, therefore, no fiery entrance as it spiralled towards a large island in the northern hemisphere.

The probe observed as much as its sensors allowed and relayed the data to its swarthy masters before they ordered it to continue its eternal vigil of the local cosmos.

The space shuttle 'Atlantis' passed within two miles of 'M/OC47', but did not even catch a glimpse of its space-black form. The pilots of the bird-like craft and most of the six billion humans of the planet Earth had no notion as to its existence. It, along with its many brothers, stood silent sentry, unknown and unrewarded.

CHAPTER ONE

"There are no unidentified flying objects skittering about our skies. There are no alien abductees. There are no extra-terrestrials visiting our planet."

The crowd in the conference hall erupted and began hurling colourful retorts at me. I had lectured at UFO symposia many times before so I was used to such abuse. I ducked as a scrunched-up programme whistled over my head.

These ufologists were so gullible. If somebody came along and said they believed that extra-terrestrials had made contact with us, then they would readily be given a platform upon which to speak, no matter how wild and outlandish their theories. This I had done many times. I would find out where major UFO conferences were being held and contact the organizers. I would tell them who I was (more often than not, the phone would be slammed down on their end at this point), that I had new evidence and that my previously sceptical viewpoint had shifted. Nine times out of ten, they would give me a small spot during the conference and I would deliver my speech.

Idiots.

"What about all the credible witnesses?"

I was pulled back to the present when an immense man in the front row stood up and lobbed his question in my general direction. He was clearly quite upset by my lecture as his face was bright red and his jowls were quivering menacingly. I gave him my best, disarmingly smug smile.

"There are no credible witnesses," I replied, the forced grin still etched onto my face.

"But policemen, airline pilots, military personnel..."

"Oh, come on. You are talking about the worst kinds of eyewitnesses. They are trained observers, yes, but they are trained to observe very specific kinds of things. How can they identify a spaceship better than any other member of the public?"

"What about photos and video evidence?" This came from several rows back.

"Fakes and misidentifications," I sighed. "And before anyone asks, the so-called abductees probably confused individuals or fraudsters. Hypnotic regression is notoriously unreliable. They are either making it all up or are weaving together parts of stories they have read or seen on television or at the cinema."

"But most of them say that they knew nothing about the UFO phenomenon."

"How can anybody know nothing about UFOs?" I was starting to get rather angry with these suggestible simpletons. "Every time you open a newspaper or turn on the television, there's some person saying that they've had an alien's baby or that they've been to Venus. Flying saucer lore is so engrained in the human psyche that anyone could engineer a convincing story and make millions out of it."

The crowd erupted again and a hail of screwed-up programmes showered onto the stage. I thanked the audience for listening, said good evening and exited stage left. I was met by Graeme Tovey, the organiser of the event. He was one of those chubby types with a head full of hair—and I mean a head full. Just about every square inch had some sort of follicular growth sprouting from it.

"You bastard," he hissed through clenched teeth.

"Steady on, Graeme," I replied jovially. "Your beard is bristling."

"Get out, Lewis!" he yelled. Then, as I headed for the door, "That's it, Lewis. You've conned us one too many times. You'll never speak at a convention again."

I turned around. "Conned us one too many times," I mimicked in a high-pitched falsetto. "That's rich! It's never stopped you listening to all the sickos and publicity-seekers out there who say that they've seen bug-eyed monsters with green scales."

"They're grey," came the quiet reply.

"Jesus Christ!" I turned back around and pushed the bar on the fire exit door.

I found myself outside the conference centre at the top of some steps that overlooked a large car park. The door slammed behind me, drowning out the hoots of outrage from within.

I looked up at the night sky and took a deep, cleansing breath. It was a cold, clear February evening and I watched as my breath drifted lazily away. There was no moon. Several thousand naked-eye stars were glittering beautifully.

As an astronomer, I appreciated what the designers of the conference centre had done with the lighting in the car park. All the lamps had wide hoods on top to prevent any light leakage above. This meant that all the light was projected towards the ground and not upwards, as was the case with most urban street lighting.

As I absorbed the awesome scope of the stellar heavens, I reached into my jacket pocket and produced a slightly crumpled pack of cigarettes. Taking one out and flicking it into my mouth (a trick I had learned at university), I replaced the pack and took out my cheap, disposable lighter. I lit the bent cigarette and inhaled its calming, poisonous fumes. I had stopped on January the first, only to start again on the second. I hadn't really wanted to stop anyway. I took another drag and exhaled, watching the smoke drift across the car park towards my battered Maestro.

I looked up again and saw a distant airliner threading its way between the stars, its lights winking at me annoyingly. I briefly wondered where it was going and what the people on board were doing at that exact moment.

Then I noticed the other plane.

It was trailing the first one, probably several miles behind, but its lights were much more dynamic. They pulsed rather than flashed—and it was quite hypnotic. A thought occurred to me, but I dismissed it hastily and tucked it away at the back of my mind where such silly notions belonged.

I watched as the two aircraft disappeared into the distance, light pollution from the nearby city of Waleford swallowing them up like some giant, ethereal child slowly gobbling up two shimmering boiled sweets.

Starting down the steps, I weaved between the parked vehicles as I made my way to my own jalopy, sitting on its own in a dark corner of the car park.

I unlocked the door and got in, stubbing out my cigarette in the overflowing ashtray. I inserted my key into the ignition and turned it. A flush of pride swept over me as the engine started immediately.

"Good girl," I muttered, patting the dashboard. "Never fails me."

Putting the car into gear and releasing the slightly wobbly handbrake, I exited the car park and headed away from the bright lights of Waleford.

Twenty-thousand feet above and several miles behind Lewis' car, the second aircraft ceased its pursuit of the airliner, executed an impossibly tight one hundred and eighty degree turn and headed in the direction of the small, blue automobile.

CHAPTER TWO

I had booked a room at the Travel Lodge that was located about ten miles outside Waleford. You might think that ten miles is a bit far to travel from the conference centre for a one-night gig, but I had learned from previous, bitter experience. A few miles between me and a mob of angry ufologists did both of our groups the world of good (mine being a group of one, of course). They got to vent their anger upon each other and I got to toast my success from my room's well-stocked mini-bar at Tovey's expense—heh heh.

As I drove down a dark country lane towards the motel, I glanced at my reflection in the rear-view mirror. My blue eyes stared back at me malevolently. I always got a fiendish thrill when appearing at one of those conventions. It was my own, small way of getting back at my ex-wife.

She was a leading ufologist (though I had not known this when we first met) and we had argued constantly about extra-terrestrial life. She was of the school that thought man was the consequence of alien genetic experimentation and that the Greys were keeping an almond eye on us. I, on the other hand, believed that the UFO/alien issue was a load of illusory codswallop.

I glanced back at the road as a fox darted in front of my car a few hundred yards ahead. Its eyes reflected my headlights briefly and then it was gone, slinking into the surrounding, swarthy fields.

I looked into the rear-view mirror again. My eyes were still there, peering back at me, but now with a hint of sadness in their liquid depths.

I had always regretted leaving Anne, but life with her had become intolerable. Towards the end, she would invite her kooky friends round for dinner. They would discuss the latest sightings over starters, cattle mutilations over the main course (which I always thought was highly distasteful, especially when they would produce graphic, full-colour photographs just as I was tucking in to my roast beef) and abductions over dessert.

Afterwards, over drinks in the lounge, the assembled nutters would get terribly excited when Anne would put on one of her favourite UFO videos and everyone, except me, would bounce up and down and gesticulate wildly at the screen.

This was when I started my career as a debunker.

In fact, Graeme Tovey was there when I initiated my first tirade. Afterwards, I had slept on the couch. Anne and I did not speak to each other for a week after that.

Six months later (and eighteen months ago), Anne and I were divorced. With no children to worry about, it went through very smoothly, even though I tried, unsuccessfully, to spin it out a bit. You see, I still loved Anne and I believe that she loved me at the time. But when your every waking hour at home is spent rowing about nonsense, something has got to give.

Unfortunately, what gave was my head when Anne hit me over it with a cheap vase.

Before blacking out, I remember being somewhat irked by the fact that it had been the vase given to us by my mother and not the cheaper, tackier one from hers, which was sitting smugly nearby. The next day, with a throbbing head, I gathered my things and left. She had stood, stone-faced, in the porch, her Roswell earrings glinting in my car's headlights as I reversed down the drive.

Those same headlights were now illuminating the lane in front of me. I studied my reflection once more. A shock of blond hair sat atop a face that had carved a niche somewhere between handsome and chiselled average. Clinging to the bottom half of that face was two days' worth of beard growth and below that sat a body that did its job—just. All in all, though, not bad for a scientist. Usually they were either obscenely overweight or looked like mops wearing white coats. I fell somewhere in between, but without the white coat.

Bill Lewis, Doctor of Astronomy at Loughfield University, part-time UFO debunker—liked by my peers, tolerated by my students and hated by just about everybody else.

I looked at my reflection again (this kind of narcissism was not common for me, but that night I was feeling particularly good about myself), more specifically at my mouth.

"It's your fault!" I blamed and my reflection said it back a trillionth of a second later.

Turning my eyes back onto the road, I saw several rabbits sitting on the grass verge, staring in my direction, their large eyes diamonds in the night. As I whizzed past, I again utilized the mirror, but this time to see if I could still catch a glimpse of the rabbits.

I should not have been able to see them once I had driven by; the lane was very dark and unlit by streetlights. But they were clearly visible behind me. They were bathed in a soft, amber glow that emanated from a pulsating ball of light that hovered about a hundred feet above the road.

I slammed my foot on the brakes and the car screeched to a juddering halt.

Craning my neck around to see out of the back window, I watched with semi-scientific fascination as the half-dozen rabbits simply sat frigid in the pool of light, their black eyes gazing vacantly ahead of them. I realized that I must have driven directly under the object and when I had passed the rodents, it had turned on its lights, obviously expecting me to carry on driving away.

I wish that I had.

"It's a helicopter," I muttered to myself. But there was no sound, only the noise of my car's engine idling to itself.

Suddenly the rabbits vanished. I blinked and rubbed my eyes. One second they were there, squatting cutely beside the road, and then they were gone. The amber light went out.

I lit a cigarette.

Rolling down the window, I stuck out my head and peered into the star-filled sky. Nothing. No planes. No helicopters. No (ha ha) flying saucers.

A shiver ran down my spine. I could envision Tovey, Anne and all the other UFO nuts laughing at me while I stood, broken and defeated, on a stage telling them about my sighting of an alien spaceship.

Then the engine cut out.

I screamed and the cigarette fell into my lap. I screamed again as a hole was burned into my new trousers. I retrieved the errant cigarette and flicked it out of the open window.

"Bugger!" I snarled and turned the key in the ignition.

Nothing happened. I felt sweat begin to bead on my forehead.

"Bugger! Bugger!" I double-snarled and tried again.

Still nothing happened. I realized that I was still about six miles from the Travel Lodge and unlike many modern, trendy scientists, I did not carry a mobile phone. I looked at my watch, squinting to see its hands in the gloom. Five past eleven.

I got out of the car and glared across the surrounding countryside, hoping to catch sight of a friendly, well-lit farmhouse or inn. No such luck. The only lights visible were from Waleford, five miles away. In a nearby field, I heard a cow mooing. Well, at least I had company of sorts. It had not even occurred to me to pop the bonnet and take a look at the engine. But, I am an astronomer not a mechanic. Besides, I didn't have a torch.

"Typical," I said to my beefy companion. "I break down equidistant from the conference centre and the Travel Lodge. Know anything about internal combustion engines?"

"Moo!"

"Thought not."

All thoughts of the mysterious light and the disappearing rabbits had gone as I mused over my current predicament.

Then I heard a faint hissing, whistling sound; like a breeze warbling through winter boughs. It seemed to surround me, yet my eyes were inexplicably drawn upwards.

High above me a huge, black triangle was eclipsing the stars. The only way that I could discern that it was a triangle was because it had bright, white lights shimmering on each of its corners.

I felt a dewdrop trickle down my leg. Great! I was going to be abducted by aliens, even possibly act as ambassador for the whole human race, and I had just peed myself! I stood transfixed as the object hovered above me, turning slowly like some insane, flying carousel.

For what seemed like minutes, but was probably only a few seconds, nothing happened. I stared, awe-struck, at the object and it stared right back at me. Again, the image of scores of ufologists ridiculing me flashed across my somewhat numbed mind. I looked down to inspect my trousers and saw that I had only the smallest of damp spots, immediately beside the hole that my rebellious cigarette had created.

Then I was surrounded by the soft, amber glow.

There was no fanfare of music or dazzling sound effects, like you see in the movies, only silence and the almost imperceptible hissing from the object above.

I looked up again, but could no longer see the craft; its form was totally obscured by the yellow light. It was then that I realized that as I had looked up, I had felt something brush against my face. An immensely velvety and pleasurable feeling. I raised my hand and drew it back and forth in front of me. It was like standing inside the most lightly-whipped banana milk shake ever created, except that there was no straw and it did not smell of bananas. The odour was more like disinfectant. Very, very strong disinfectant. In fact, that was the only unpleasant part of the experience so far. The caress of the glow made me feel extremely relaxed and I could quite easily have pulled the light around me, like a soft blanket, rolled up on the ground and fallen fast asleep.

I did not get the chance.

There was an eye-stinging flash and the glow vanished.

Actually, everything vanished; the road, my car, the countryside were all gone. I was lying on a cold, hard surface in the middle of a brilliantly-lit room, facing the ceiling. I assume that it was a room as everywhere was equally bright and I could not make out where the walls, floor and ceiling started or finished.

I tried to sit up, but discovered, to my horror, that I was paralysed. All feeling throughout my body below the neck had somehow been severed. Fear began to take a grip and adrenalin rushed along my inert capillaries. As if by some minute consolation, I found that I could turn my head and look to either side of the table.

I peered to the left and saw my clothes lying in an untidy pile on what I presumed was the floor. To the right was another table upon which were my friends, the rabbits. Unfortunately for them, they also appeared to be paralysed and had dozens of strange-looking instruments protruding from their abdomens. I tried to look closer and saw that the devices were inserted into large incisions that had been cut into the animals' bellies.

I felt bile rise in my throat.

Then movement made me look more closely at one of the rodents. It turned its head and stared straight at me, abject terror in its dark eyes. They were still alive! Then a terrible thought struck me. I lifted my head as far as I could and glanced down at my own torso.

Similar devices projected from my own splayed belly.

I screamed, I think. No sound carried in the room. I tried again, but to no avail. A final attempt proved equally fruitless. With no way to vent my self-pervading panic, I banged my head back down onto the table beneath me, wincing as pain shot around my cranium. At least I had some feeling left. That was a start.

Out of the brightness stepped three small figures. They approached the table that held the rabbits and busied themselves by removing the instruments from the creatures' bodies. I called out voicelessly. They must have heard me, because one of them turned around and looked directly at me. Those huge, slanting, black eyes surrounded by its massive, grey head sent a chill of terror coursing through me, the likes of which I had never felt before.

Then it smiled at me. Before I could think of anything else to do, I found myself smiling back at the monstrosity. It turned back to its colleagues and continued its task with the rabbits.

When they had finished, there was a bright flash, even more luminous than the rest of the room, and they stepped back from the table.

The rabbits were gone.

I watched with horror as they turned to me. Unable to move my arms and legs, I began thrashing my head from side to side in a primitive display of utter terror. My eyes squeezed tight shut and tears rolled down my face and into my useless ears. Then a softness touched my mind, feathering my frontal lobe like a fan-dancer. A relaxing, sultry voice, neither male nor female, spoke inside my head.

"Relax. You are in no danger. You will feel no pain. The One watches over us."

I opened my eyes to see the first creature standing over me, that reassuring smile, a thin crescent, still etched onto its gaunt face. Then a slight movement caught my attention and I looked down to see an enormous hypodermic syringe in its four-fingered hand. I faced the alien and saw that the smile had been replaced by a cold, emotionless stare. Pressure between my ribs informed me that the needle had been jabbed into my right side. My whole body went numb and my vision failed with alarming speed. As there was no sound in the room to start with, I did not know if my hearing had abandoned me as well, but I could perceive the aliens' soft voices chatting in my mind.

"The specimen is ready."

"Catalogue it number 9426517."

"Proceed with organ removal and fluid extraction."

That made me sit up and take notice; metaphorically speaking, of course. I felt gentle tugs at my body.

"It hears us."

"Have no concern. Replace the specimen's organs and catalogue the fluid samples."

"Removing probes." More gentle tugs.

"Storage reports that there are no more empty tanks." I was certain that I heard a disgruntled sigh.

"Very well. Tag it, seal the opening and eject the specimen with its garments."

"Prepare the samples for the galley, the donor has arrived."

I thought that I heard the lowing of a cow in the background, but dismissed this as implausible because my ears were not working.

Can you hear me? Here I am being disembowelled by creatures from God-knows-where and I'm trying to analyse it scientifically!

Suddenly, I was sitting in my car with my trousers on back to front and my wedding ring (which I had been unable to remove for two years due to water retention) on the wrong finger. The car was surrounded by the amber glow and, looking out of my still open window, I could see the six rabbits hopping about merrily on the grass verge.

Then the light went out. I, climbed out of the car and looked upwards apprehensively.

The triangle was moving away slowly, its course taking it over the adjacent fields. There was no sound whatsoever. As I watched, the amber glow appeared again, but this time in the middle of the nearest area of pasture, where my friendly cow had been. A searing flash was followed by the introduction of a disembowelled heifer. The light winked out and the object rocketed skyward, leaving me, six unperturbed rodents and one unhappily steaming, bovine corpse.

My car engine started up then and immediately stalled. I had left it in gear. The sudden, almost ear-splitting noise in the otherwise silent lane startled me and I felt more dewdrops. I climbed into my car, slipped it into neutral and turned the key.

The engine started first time.

I put my foot hard down on the accelerator and roared off towards the Travel Lodge, hatching a scheme to sneak by the receptionist without her seeing me in such a state.

As I disappeared in a cloud of dust, the rabbits continued their business on the verge, seemingly none the worse for wear after their ordeal.

CHAPTER THREE

Luckily, I discovered that the gents' toilets were in the motel's reception lobby before one reached the check-in desk. I was able to dash in there, put my trousers on properly and generally try to tidy myself up a little. I felt in my jacket pocket for my cigarettes, but found that they were missing. I supposed that they had been taken by my alien captors.

Good, I hope you all get cancer, I thought vengefully.

Exiting the toilets, I strolled casually up to the receptionist, failing miserably to hide the damp spot and cigarette burn near my groin. She was a young woman of about twenty and quite attractive too.

"Can I help you, sir?" She had difficulty tearing her eyes away from my genital area. That was a first for me, I can tell you.

"Er, yes. I believe you have a reservation for William Lewis. A Mister Tovey arranged it."

She studied her notepad, obviously grateful for the distraction, and by the look on her face, I feared the worst.

"I'm sorry, Mister Lewis, but Mister Tovey rang a couple of hours ago and cancelled the reservation."

"A couple of hours? But I only left the conference centre half an hour ago." I glanced at the clock behind the reception desk, and then at my watch, which was now on my right wrist as opposed to its regular home on my left one. Both timepieces said that it was one thirty in the morning. I stood and flustered for a few seconds and the girl must have taken pity on me, considering my dishevelled appearance.

"Have you had an accident?"

"Yes, I think I have—Oh, you mean in the car. No," I read the name on her lapel badge. "Denise. No, my car broke down. It must have taken me longer to fix it than I thought. I'm very tired." I yawned, wildly exaggerating the action.

"Look, the room is still empty," said Denise, her lilting tones caressing my ears like butterfly wings. "If you want it, it's yours."

"You are an angel," I gushed.

"That'll be twenty four ninety five for the night." Her halo shattered.

I grudgingly took out my wallet and flipped three ten pound notes onto the counter. Signing the book, I collected my change and accepted the chalet key from Denise de Sade. As I turned to leave the lobby, I asked if the room had a phone.

"Yes, just dial nine and then your number. You'll be billed when you check out."

"Thanks, Sadie," I said as I scurried outside.

I crossed the car park to my room and inserted the key in the door lock. I noticed that I had been given the chalet farthest from the reception block, tucked away between some bushes and the laundry room. Well, at least I would get some peace and quiet.

The door swung open and I stepped inside the distastefully furnished room. The walls were painted that horrible off-beige colour that semi-disguises vomit stains. Fortunately, my room had no such blotches; it was clean and the single bed beckoned to me invitingly.

I decided that I could not be bothered to get my things from the car and belly-flopped spectacularly onto the mattress. It was then that I realized that the cabin door had been left wide open. I struggled to my feet, with not inconsiderable effort, and crossed the puke-coloured carpet to the draughty entrance.

I was just about to slam it shut when a tall man wearing a black pin-stripe suit appeared in front of me. I was so startled by his sudden arrival that I shrieked aloud. Behind him was an equally lofty man in an equally black suit. Both men wore wide-brimmed hats that were of the same dye as their suits and I was briefly of the opinion that they were Quakers. From the configuration of their faces, I got the impression that they were brothers, if not twins. Duelling Banjos played silently in my mind.

"Doctor Lewis?" the foremost one asked flatly.

"Yes, I'm Lewis," I yawned. He removed his hat to reveal a closely shaved, almost bald, blond head.

"Doctor Lewis, my associate and I are from the Ministry of Defence." His eyes seemed to be tunnelling through my skull, as though he could get to any secrets locked inside my brain by will power alone. "We have learned that you may have had an unusual encounter this evening."

Suddenly, Anne's stories about the Men-In-Black leaped into my mind. Mysterious, dark-garbed people, pretending to be government officials, who appeared almost immediately following some poor sod's UFO encounter. Nobody knew who they were. Some said that they genuinely were government agents from some top-secret department. Others said that they were aliens disguised as humans. A few said that they were human/alien hybrids, bred by the Greys to infiltrate human society. Many said that they were a mixture of all the above.

I always said that it was a load of rot. Until tonight. If these two Cro-Magnons were not MIBs then I was Buck Rogers.

You may have guessed by now that my debunking days were well and truly behind me. It went completely against the grain for me, but the events of the evening had left my concept of reality spinning like a politician's press secretary.

I felt like I had tumbled into a mighty quicksilver river, its frictionless current sweeping me effortlessly along its course. I knew that as I travelled these mercury rapids, strange and disturbing truths would be constantly, inexorably presented to my reeling intellect.

"I don't know what you're talking about," I lied.

"May we come in, Doctor Lewis?" It was not really a question and he took a step closer.

"Have you any ID?"

"Why are you being so uncooperative, Doctor Lewis?"

Something inside me snapped. Maybe it was the stress of recent events catching up with me; maybe it was the fact that I had not had a cigarette for over two hours. Or maybe it was just the fact that I did not particularly like these two pinstriped freaks. They acted like the traffic cop whom has just pulled you over at three in the morning for no reason and proceeds to speak to you like you've just had major brain surgery.

"Look," I said loudly. "I am very tired and I want to go to sleep. If you're not going to show me any identification, then I am going to slam this door in your face." I waited for two seconds. "No ID? Good night."

I shoved the door to slam it. However, the Man-In-Black stopped it before it closed.

"Doctor Lewis, do not talk to anybody about your encounter tonight. If you do, you will regret it."

"Is that a threat?"

"Yes."

Then they were gone. They climbed into a huge, black car (a model that I was unfamiliar with) and drove silently into the night.

I closed the door and crossed the room to the bed. I began to tremble and had to sit down as an uncontrollable shaking fit possessed me. Delayed shock is a terrible thing. After a minute or two, the shakes ebbed and I sat with my head in a pair of sweaty palms. I thought that I was going to be all right until I darted into the bathroom and threw up in the sink.

When the retching subsided, I rinsed my face with cold water and looked at my sorry reflection in the bathroom mirror. I had definitely shifted into the average looks' niche. Dark circles had appeared beneath my eyes and I had three ugly bruises on my forehead—one on each side, just above the temples and one smack in the middle, between my eyebrows.

Images of my ordeal filtered into the haze of my memory and before I knew what I was doing, I was pulling off my jacket and unbuttoning my shirt. I was expecting to see a horrendous scar with huge, alien stitches going the length of my torso.

Imagine my surprise when all I could make out was a faint red line stretching from just below my rib cage to my navel. As I inspected my belly, the line faded and soon there was no evidence of my abduction, save for the bruises on my head and my absurdly vivid memory of the horror.

I washed my face again and looked once more at my hideous reflection. The bruises were gone, vanished as if the cold water had sluiced them down the plughole. The dark, moon-shaped circles under my eyes were as prominent as ever, though.

I rushed into the bedroom and scooped up the phone. I hit the nine button and realized that I had left my jacket on the bathroom floor. Replacing the receiver, I dashed into the other room and riffled through the pockets of my coat. Finding my organiser, I raced back to the bed, flipping through the pages of phone numbers as I sat down. Locating Tovey's number and dialling it, I listened as it rang at the other end. Then there were two clicks and the ringing started again.

"This is the Committee of Citizens' Knowledge of Unexplained Phenomena office. I am afraid that the office is closed right now, but if you would like to leave your name, number and a short message, please speak after the tone."

A second later, the beep sounded and I recorded my message. "Graeme, it's Bill Lewis. I need to speak to you and Anne. I'll be home tomorrow, so please call me. And for what it's worth—I'm sorry about what I did at the convention."

I doubted that Tovey would call me back after what had transpired earlier, but if Anne heard the message, then I was sure that she would contact me.

I smiled as I remembered the time when Tovey, Anne and several others had set up the Committee of Citizens' Knowledge of Unexplained Phenomena. I had guffawed most uncouthly as I pointed out that the group's acronym was C.O.C.K.U.P. But they had kept the name nevertheless and nobody else seemed to notice the hilarious arrangement of capitals. Or at least they did not comment if they did.

My smile turned into a grimace as I realized that C.O.C.K.U.P. was my only hope. Only they had the necessary experience in these matters and only they could help me. If I could not secure their aid, then I was certain that I would surely go crazy.

I replaced the receiver and almost jumped out of my skin when the phone rang jarringly a few seconds later. Picking it up, I spoke gingerly into the mouthpiece.

"Hello?"

"Mister Lewis?" It was Denise, the receptionist from Hades. "Do you own a light blue Maestro?"

"Yes, it's parked by reception. Why?"

"I think you'd better come and take a look at it." I was sure that there was a hint of wicked glee in her voice. Or maybe I was becoming paranoid.

Pulling on my shirt and jacket, I left the cabin, locking the door behind me, and strode purposefully towards the reception block. As I neared the car, my purposeful stride became an awkward gait and by the time I reached it, my gait had disintegrated into a dejected stagger.

All four tyres had been slashed, the side windows had been shattered and the words GIT and ARSEHOLE had been crudely spray-painted onto the doors and bonnet.

"Quite a mess, Mister Lewis." I turned to see Denise and a young man in similar colours approaching cautiously.

"Didn't you hear anything?" I demanded angrily. This was all I needed. I could quite easily have had a nervous breakdown right on the spot. Luckily I am made of sterner stuff. But only just.

Denise shot a nervous glance at the young man, who was shuffling about awkwardly. "Sorry, Mister Lewis, but me and Pete were, er, busy."

I looked at Pete, who was still treading the ground with his feet, but now he had a smile on his face that threatened to push his ears round to the back of his head. "Yeah, I bet you were," was all I said.

"I called the police as soon as I saw it," stated Denise, attempting to save face on her embarrassing predicament. "They said they were coming straight over."

Right on cue, headlights appeared at the motel gate and a single, white police car pulled up beside my ravaged vehicle. Two officers got out and began to inspect the damage. The elder of the two shook his head in dismay, but his younger partner took one look at the graffiti and smirked into his hand.

"That's enough, Willis."

"Sorry, Sarge."

"Is this your car, sir?" asked the sergeant from over the roof of my abused automobile. I nodded as he took out his notebook. "Name, sir?" I told him and added my address as well. "Willis, call it in and run a check." He looked back at me. "Just routine, Doctor Lewis. I'm sure you understand."

"Yes, of course," I replied miserably.

The police officer rubbed the back of his neck and grimaced at my wrecked baby. "Do you have any idea who could have done this?"

I knew perfectly well who was responsible for the desecration of my beautiful wheels. That was why Tovey's answering machine was turned on. He always answered the phone at night and only used the machine when he was out during the day. Graeme had obviously raised a posse and hunted me down. Of course, being geeky wimps, they did not beat down my door and kick the crap out of me. No, they took out their collective frustration on my beloved car, which was probably crueler than knocking the stuffing out of me. At least I would have healed; it was going to cost me a fortune to repair the shambles squatting in front of me. Unfortunately for me, but luckily for him, I needed Tovey right now.

"No, sergeant. It's a mystery to me."

"I see." He jotted down some notes (probably something along the lines of lying sod!) and turned to Pete and Denise. "What about you two. See or hear anything?"

"Er, no, Sergeant Hawkins. We were stock-taking in the back room," replied Denise. The policeman looked to Pete for confirmation. He simply nodded and started shuffling again.

Willis called over from the patrol car. "Doctor Lewis checks out, Sarge. It's his car all right."

"Okay. Thanks, Willis." He turned back to me. "Well, sir. I don't think there's anything more we can do here. Can we call a tow truck for you?"

"No thanks, I've got breakdown cover." This brought a raised eyebrow from Denise. "I'll call the AA and have them take it to the local garage."

"I'm sure your insurance will cover the damage, sir."

"Yeah," I sighed. "Doesn't make it any easier though, does it?"

"No, I don't suppose it does." Hawkins slipped the notebook back into his breast pocket. "Well, we'll make the usual enquiries and if anything turns up, we'll be in touch."

"Thanks, sergeant."

With that, the two policemen climbed back into their car and drove away. I turned to Denise, whose eyebrows were still raised.

"Why didn't you call the AA when your car broke down earlier, Doctor Lewis?"

She emphasized my title and folded her arms across her ample bosom.

"I didn't call them because I was in the middle of bloody nowhere, Miss Marple." I spun round, stalked back towards my cabin, spun again, stalked back, grabbed the bag from the back seat of my car and slouched off to my room.

From there, I called the breakdown service and arranged for someone to pick up my car and tow it to the nearest garage. A long, hot shower revived me a little, the powerful spray doing wonders for my mood. Once my nightclothes had been donned (shorts and T-shirt), I called the reception desk and instructed Denise to have me woken when the breakdown truck arrived in the morning. She promised that she would pass on the message and then, to my surprise, apologized sincerely for her earlier behaviour. I forgave her and hung up. Told you I was in a better mood.

I climbed into bed and snuggled up under the covers, leaving all the lights on. I was still feeling a little paranoid, despite the shower, so I got out of bed and double-checked the window and door fastenings. Satisfied that they were securely locked, I clambered back beneath the sheets.

With my emotions in such a jumbled, delicate state, I began thinking all sorts of strange, unpleasant thoughts. Then I sat bolt upright.

The phone.

Each time I had used it, there had been two strange clicks before I got through. Or had I imagined it? I decided to test my hypothesis and picked up the receiver. I dialled the number for my own house and the phone rang for a couple of seconds. Then two loud clicks interrupted the ringing before the double tones continued. I hung up.

"The phones are bugged," I whispered to myself, pulling the cover up under my chin and peering anxiously around the room. Perhaps the whole place was wired, I thought and curled up into a tight ball beneath the sheets.

Thoughts of secret agents and governmental conspiracies clogged my cerebral pathways.

I soon fell asleep and was instantly assailed by dreams of me standing naked on a stage while Tovey, Anne and millions of their friends laughed and threw rotten fruit at me as I tried to explain my change of heart and that I now believed whole-heartedly in unidentified flying objects.

It was the worst night's sleep of my life. At least things could not get any worse—or so I thought.

CHAPTER FOUR

The next day started as the previous one had finished—badly.

After a restless night, I was summoned from my bed at eight o'clock when the breakdown man arrived. Denise had finished work at six and was replaced by a gangly youth with the worst case of acne that I had ever seen. Why the hell didn't the management put him on the night shift and the lovely Denise on days?

As the truck driver pulled the car onto the back of his flatbed, I paid my bill at the reception desk.

"... and your phone bill comes to ten pounds thirty, sir."

"What?" I cried. The youth almost died with fright. I read his nametag. "Look, Steve, I've only been here for one night. How can my phone bill be over ten pounds?"

Stevie Hut produced a sheaf of computer printout and brandished it defensively. "It's all right here, sir, in black and white."

I snatched the forms from him and scrutinized them fiercely, occasionally rewarding the trembling receptionist with an Arctic stare. Unfortunately, he was correct. Somehow my phone bill had come to ten pounds and thirty pence. Unbelievably, I had been charged for the call to my house—when I had not even received a reply. In fact, this call seemed to take up the majority of the total bill. I pointed this out to Steve, who merely shrugged and said that I must have left the phone off the hook all night. I stated that I had not even got through to my last number, but he just shrugged again (I was beginning to dislike this spotty little creep immensely) and proclaimed that the billing starts as soon as the receiver is picked up.

I was just considering stuffing the bill down his scrawny, anorexic neck when the AA man entered the lobby and informed me that he was ready to leave. I grudgingly paid the phone bill and gave Steve a scathing glare as I left with the tow-truck driver.

As we crossed the car park to his waiting behemoth, the driver turned his head in my direction and spoke in overly cheerful tones.

"I've called Jobsons in Waleford, Mister Lewis. They say that they can replace your tyres and windows by lunchtime. I don't know what they'll be able to do with the paintwork, though."

"We'll just have to see what happens." I spied a packet of cigarettes in his overall pocket. My nicotine gland started salivating. "Could you spare me one of those? I haven't had one all night."

"Well, I'm not supposed to smoke except on my breaks."

"I won't tell."

He reached into his pocket and passed me the pack and a box of matches. I took one out, lit it and inhaled deeply, a pleasant dizziness swimming over me.

"Thanks," I said, handing the boxes back to him.

We climbed into his rig and soon were trundling down the lane towards the city. As we approached the area where I had experienced my trauma, I felt the hairs on the back of my neck begin to prickle. I started puffing on a second, kindly-donated cigarette like I was standing before a firing squad.

"Are you all right, mate?" asked the driver genuinely.

Activity in a nearby field drew my attention away from his enquiry. As we drove on, I saw a police car parked by a gate in the dry-stone wall bordering the meadow and Sergeant Hawkins, Constable Willis and a man whom I presumed to be a farmer could be seen inspecting something lying in the grass. Another man buzzed around the trio, taking numerous photographs of whatever they were looking at.

"What's going on over there?"

The driver followed the line of my finger and slowed the truck so that we could obtain a clearer view. "Ah, that must be what Harry was going on about."

"Who?"

"Harry at Jobsons." He stated this as though only an idiot would not know of Harry at Jobsons. "He said that he heard on the local radio that a farmer found one of his cows and a few of his sheep mysteriously butchered in a field not far from the Travel Lodge."

"I wouldn't exactly call six miles not far," I proffered.

He looked at me out of the corner of his good eye. "You know what I mean. Anyhow, according to Harry, most of the cow's organs had been removed with surgical precision and not a drop of blood has been found near the carcass. Well, that's what he said the radio said. He said there must be some real nutters about. Meself, I think it's all these yoofoes that people have been seeing."

My head whipped round so sharply to face him that I thought it would keep on going and do a full three hundred and sixty degrees. "What did you say?"

"I know it sounds loony," he continued. "But I saw it on the telly. Aliens take cows and stuff, cut 'em up for experiments and that and then just drop the bodies out of their spaceships as they fly past. God knows what they want 'em for."

"Maybe they just like the taste of beef," I offered quietly.

"Yeah, maybe it's just that," he laughed. "You're a genius, Mister Lewis. You a doctor or something?"

"Yes."

"Oh."

We soon left the gory scene far behind and a few minutes later we were winding our way through the bustling streets of Waleford. Eventually, we pulled up outside an impressively clean automobile repair garage with the name HARRY JOBSON'S painted in huge, white letters above the repair bays. The driver and I climbed out of the truck and crossed the forecourt to be intercepted by a greying, middle-aged man in greasy overalls.

"Morning, Bill," he said as he approached. At first I thought that he knew me from somewhere, until I realized that he was addressing the AA man. "Is this a vandalism job?"

"Yep, it certainly is, Harry. Give us a hand to unload her, will you?"

As the two men set about removing my car from its ten-wheeled stretcher, I shuffled about and gazed blankly around like you always seem to do at auto repair shops. When my car was safely on the ground, the Harry and Bill Show came back over to me. Harry eyed me up and down like virtually all mechanics seem trained to do. Bill stepped forward with a clipboard filled with multi-coloured forms.

"Right then, Mister Lewis. If you'll just sign these, I'll leave you in Harry's capable hands." I initialed the proffered sheets and handed the clipboard back to the AA man. He gave me a copy of each form and stuck his pen behind his ear. "Okay then, that's it. Watch out, Harry. He's a doctor."

With this mystifying statement, Bill leaped into his wagon and pulled out into the heaving traffic.

"Last year, I got trapped underneath a doctor's car when the jack collapsed," explained the mechanic, still eyeing me suspiciously. "Right, let's get old Betsy into the bay. There's a coffee machine in the office if you want one."

I handed him my car keys and shuffled off in the direction he was pointing, feeling somewhat like a naughty schoolboy being dismissed by the headmaster. I was halfway down my first cup of Castrol GTX when Harry popped his head around the office door.

"Mister Lewis?" I looked up from my immensely uncomfortable seat. "The tyres and windows'll be easy enough to fix, but that grafitti'll need a full respray to cover it properly. That'll cost a fair bit and it'll take time too."

I peered at him dolefully and asked if there was any way that he could just cover it up. He stood and thought for a moment, then stated that he could obliterate the profanity with a couple of coats of black spray-paint. He informed me that it would not look pretty, though.

"Well, anything's better than driving around with ARSEHOLE printed in large, purple letters on the side of my car."

He agreed and vanished as he set about his tasks.

After three more cups of motor oil and a sandwich filled with old brake linings, Harry re-entered the office, wiping his hands with a filthy rag. He stepped behind the counter and began tapping figures into the small computer terminal perched there.

After a while, he smiled and I felt like a heretic standing before the Grand Inquisitor. I half expected him to produce a ducking stool and force me to abandon Satan. He pressed a key and a printer began chattering away in the corner of the room. After what seemed like an eternity, the printer stopped and Harry tore the receipt along its perforations with a victorious flourish. I stood up and crossed to the counter. Harry placed the bill in front of me so that I could fully appreciate the enormity of the figures involved.

My knees buckled and I felt a deep rumbling in my lower bowel.

I pulled out my chequebook and began filling in the amounts, hoping that the box provided would be big enough. I signed it and reluctantly handed the leaf over to Torquemada Jobson. He accepted it gleefully and suggested that my insurance company would probably refund my outlay. I desperately hoped so.

When the ugly business had been concluded, Harry led me out of the office and onto the forecourt, where my healed baby awaited. I stopped in my tracks when I saw her.

Harry had done a terrific job. He had expertly sprayed over Tovey's handiwork with black paint, the neat, obscuring rectangles giving her the appearance of a rally car. All that was required to complete the illusion was some large sponsors' logos, some bold numbering and a three litre, ten million horsepower engine.

This was the only pleasant thing that I had experienced all that day. Believe me, worse was to come.

I thanked Harry for his sterling work, retrieved my car keys and set off for home at last.

I was too elated at having my car back in working order to notice the large, black automobile pulling out into the traffic several cars behind me. I also did not realize that this same car followed me all the way home.

Two hours and a hundred miles later, I was turning the key in my front door as the sun sank beneath the horizon and darkness soon enveloped the small cottage that I called home.

CHAPTER FIVE

Upon entering my home, I tossed the keys onto the small table by the door and flicked the light switch immediately above it. Brilliant, unshaded light displayed the full majesty of my abode. I took a deep, satisfying breath of stale air and waded through the dust to my television. I switched it on and a BBC newsreader greeted me.

The main headlines were the usual stuff; more trouble in the Middle East and the almost obligatory cabinet minister scandals.

I took off my jacket and threw it onto the couch, knocking over a large stack of essays that I had not yet marked. Ignoring them, I trudged into the kitchen, switched on the light, filled the kettle and plugged it in. I could still hear the newscaster telling himself all about the Bank of England's latest interest rate rise as I washed out a mug and scooped a teaspoonful of coffee into its stained interior. As the kettle boiled, an Opposition MP began a lengthy character assassination of the Chancellor of the Exchequer and I poured the scalding water into my mug.

Not bothering to stir it, I returned to the living room, set the coffee down on my aptly named coffee table (you had to see the multitude of hard coffee rings to catch my drift) and flopped into my favourite armchair.

I reached across and grabbed my jacket from its resting place on the couch. A quick fumble in its pockets reminded me that I had not purchased any more cigarettes. Making a life or death decision, I stood up, pulled on my coat and headed for the front door. As I left for the newsagent's, I learned that Arsenal had beaten Manchester United two nil at Highbury.

As I strolled, whistling, down the garden path, I scarcely noticed the black car parked on the opposite side of the road from my cottage. Closing the gate behind me, I headed right and trotted the hundred yards or so to Patel's Paper Shop.

"Evening, Doctor Lewis," greeted Elyas Patel, without a trace of accent, as I entered his spotless establishment. "Your usuals?"

"Yes, please," I replied. "And a loaf of bread as well?"

"Behind you."

I looked around and grabbed a loaf from the shelf at my rear. I placed it onto the counter and reached into my trouser pocket, pulling out a handful of change.

"Your wife was in here earlier, Doctor Lewis." I almost dropped the money.

"Did she say anything?" I asked, slightly taken aback.

"Just that she was looking for you. That's three sixty four, please."

I paid him and asked if anybody else had been with her. He shook his head and dropped the money into the till with an expert's touch.

"Okay. Thanks, Elyas." Before I left, I bought a box of matches and, as I walked home, I puffed nervously on a cancer stick.

I was halfway down a second cigarette when I passed through my open gate and shuffled up to my front door. I noticed that the black car had gone, but it didn't register on my befuddled synapses.

I unlocked the door, entered and sank back into my armchair. The local news had started and I watched absently as some minor duchess opened an adventure playground for under-privileged kids in Stockley.

Whilst sitting in the chair, I tugged fitfully at my jacket until it came off. I chucked it onto the couch, knocking over a neat pile of essays that I had not yet marked.

Hang on, I thought. I could have sworn that I had demolished that particular pile earlier. The next news item caught my attention and the unruly stack was forgotten.

It concerned the farmer whom I had seen earlier inspecting his mutilated heifer. The local newsman used sombre tones to inform me that the farmer had committed suicide after finding three of his herd and most of his sheep mysteriously butchered.

A CID officer appeared on the screen and began speaking in stilted policese. A caption flashed up telling me that his name was Detective Sergeant Robert McCloud of the Waleford Metropolitan Police.

"We are taking this incident very seriously," he said, stating the patently obvious. "Whoever is responsible for the mutilation of Mr. Biggins' animals will, when apprehended, be charged with the manslaughter of Mr. Biggins himself. We have an incident room set up at Waleford Police Station and will welcome any information from members of the public." "I understand that the last people to see Mr. Biggins alive were two of your patrol officers. Is there any truth in that?"

"Er, yes, that is correct."

I sat and watched with morbid fascination. The detective began squirming like a fish on a hook; the reporter had obviously asked the wrong question. I loved it when they did that. Behind him, an ambulance was pulling out of the farmyard in which he was standing. Its departure revealed a black, official-looking car parked some yards farther back.

My head shot forward as I recognized the two suited men who had threatened me the night before. They were standing by their vehicle and gazing around the muddy farmyard, their eyes hidden behind black sunglasses. I stubbed out my cigarette as the detective continued his statement.

"Mr. Biggins called out our officers this morning when he discovered the first of his animals' carcasses. Unfortunately ... "

The phone rang and I almost kicked over the coffee table in fright. I stood up and crossed the room to the windowsill, where my telephone lived. My sorry reflection gazed at me as Anne's voice spoke into my right ear.

"Bill? It's Anne."

"Hello, Anne. You got my message then?" I drew the curtains with my free hand, obliterating my translucent doppelganger. "Where's Graeme?"

"He's here. You brought it all on yourself, you know," she said regarding my conduct at the convention. I felt anger begin to rise from the pit of my stomach.

"That doesn't give him and his cronies the right to trash my car!"

"You said that you needed to talk to us, Bill. I didn't call to argue with you."

I counted to ten, then recited the Greek alphabet in my head until the rage had subsided back into the void of my grumbling stomach. Then I heard two clicks on the line, sounding like a report in the silence.

My mind wandered back to the stack of essays. Then three other pieces fell into place in the jigsaw of my memory. I had closed the gate when going to the newsagent's. The black car had been there. When I had returned, the gate was open and the car was gone.

The bastards had been in my home!

A dizzying wave of dread washed over me as I recalled the news report concerning the farmer's so-called suicide and the Man-In-Black's threatening attitude at the Travel Lodge.

"Look, Anne, can I come over and talk to you two?"

"Is everything okay, Bill? You sound scared."

"Can I come over or not?"

"Yes, of course."

"Are you at Graeme's?"

"No, we're at my house."

"Oh," I said, an unexpected twang of jealousy causing my heart to miss a beat.

"We're divorced, Bill."

"Forget it, I'm on my way over." I was about to put down the receiver, when something occurred to me. "Anne?"

"Yes?"

"When you came over earlier, did you leave your house empty?"

"No, I got some total strangers to house-sit for me—of course I left it empty! What are you trying to say?"

"I'll meet you and Graeme in the Plough and tell him it doesn't matter about the car. I forgive him."

I slammed down the phone, gathered my jacket and keys and rushed out of the door, leaving the lights and television on. I did not even bother to lock the door after me. What was the point? I thought. If they wanted to get in, then a locked door was not going to stop them.

I dove into my car, started up the engine and gunned the accelerator. With a screech of agonized tyres, I raced away and headed for the neighbouring town of Stockley.

My car roared through the village and began roaring more vehemently as I joined the dual carriageway that led to the nearest urban centre. I glanced upwards nervously and saw that dark clouds had gathered overhead. Small spots of rain began to burst onto the glass, closely followed by larger, more substantial raindrops. I turned on my wipers and watched as they drew perfect arcs in front of me. Then I remembered to switch on my headlights. I passed several cars during the course of my journey and only ten minutes later, I zipped by a nondescript sign that declared that I was entering the town of Stockley. A slow drive through the still reasonably busy town centre, followed by a right and two left turns brought me onto the street upon which the Plough Inn had been built some two hundred years ago.

I pulled into the small car park and saw Tovey's Land Rover sitting quietly by a rain-soaked table. I considered getting out a screwdriver and wreaking sweet revenge on his paintwork, but thought better of it. I brought my car to a halt beside his ungainly beast and got out. Icy rain speckled my face and I dashed into the invitingly lit pub.

Seeing Anne and a nervous-looking Tovey sitting in the far corner of the Tap Room, I ordered a pint of bitter from the corpulent landlord and crossed to join them.

"Hello, Anne. Graeme."

"Hello, Bill," replied Anne, a stern look on her pretty, oval face. It was framed by her trademark long, brown hair and I suppressed a smile as I noticed that she was wearing her Roswell earrings. "Please, sit down."

"Thanks." I perched on a stool opposite the ufologists and smiled at Tovey.

"Lewis," he greeted gruffly.

"Doesn't this guy know my first name yet?" I queried jovially.

"Don't start, Bill," countered my ex-wife. "What do you want to talk to us about? And why all this cloak and dagger stuff?"

"Right," I began and took a mighty swig from my glass. I looked over my shoulder towards the door, half expecting dozens of government agents to come bursting in and slam hundreds of silenced bullets into my back. I started as the door opened, but only an old man in a flat cap and his Jack Russell entered. "Before I start, I'd better tell you that I've had a change of heart."

"Not another one?" sneered Tovey. I shot him an angry look and, to my surprise, so did Anne.

"I know that you've no reason to believe me," I continued unperturbed. "But what I am about to tell you is absolutely true." I took another long draught of my ale. "Did you see the news report about the mutilated cattle near Waleford?" "Yes," replied Tovey, leaning forward slightly. "We tried sending a team in to document the incident, but the police told us to sling our collective hooks."

"Well, I think I know who killed him."

"The police said that it was suicide," said Anne.

"And I know what happened to his animals," I finished. I drained the last of my bitter, watching Anne and

Tovey exchange suspicious glances through the bottom of my glass. I placed the empty beaker on the table and made sure that I had their total attention. Then I informed them of my experience in the country lane the night before. I recounted the tale as accurately as I could remember and sat back as they stared at me with wide eyes.

"I don't believe you, Lewis," said Tovey a few seconds later. "As I said at the conference centre, you've done this kind of thing too many times before. Have you ever read The Boy Who Cried Wolf?"

"If it's not true, then why am I being followed? Why was my motel room bugged—and my own house? Why was I threatened by two mysterious men claiming to be from the Ministry Of Defence? Those same two men who I saw at the Biggins Farm."

"So you say. It's just like you said at the convention," came Tovey's reply. "UFO lore is so engrained in the human psyche that anybody could fabricate a credible story and dupe all of us."

"Looks like I've hung a noose around my own neck, doesn't it?" I looked to Anne. She was peering into the bottom of her gin and tonic. "What about you? I suppose you think I'm making it all up as well, don't you?"

"Look, Bill." She raised her head, a sorrowful expression on her face. "Graeme's right. This isn't the first time that you've come to us saying that you've been converted."

"But this time I'm telling you the truth!" I stood up, almost knocking the table over. "I'm telling you that I, William Lewis PhD, have been abducted by aliens!"

The pub fell into silence and all eyes turned on me. A young woman at a nearby table giggled and her boyfriend gave me a threatening scowl. I slowly sat back down and the hum of conversation gradually returned to a normal level. No doubt I was the new topic of discussion—the loony who talks to Martians. I checked to make sure that I still had my clothes on. “Can you help me or not?” I asked quietly.

“What do you expect us to do?” replied Tovey, disbelief still evident in his eyes.

“I don’t know! You’re the bloody experts!” I shouted.

“Right, that’s it,” called the landlord as he pulled another pint for the man in the flat cap. “One more word out of you and you’re barred.”

I searched for Anne and Tovey’s support, but they just peered into their laps like ostriches burying their heads in the proverbial sand. I stood up and glared down at them.

“Well, thanks a lot for your compassion. If you won’t help me, then I suppose I’ll just have to help myself.” I turned to leave, the whole pub watching me again.

“Bill, wait,” Anne called, but I was already out of the door and striding angrily towards my waiting car. The freezing rain pouring down the back of my neck didn’t help my mood much, either.

I unlocked the door and climbed in, slamming it so hard that the window rattled dangerously. I sat there for a full minute, dripping onto the steering wheel, before starting the engine. I looked back and began reversing the car out of its parking space when a figure appeared in my path. I slammed on the brakes and dived out of the car, taking the keys with me. Before me stood Anne, soaked and bedraggled in the downpour.

“What the hell do you think you’re doing?” I yelled and lightning flashed as if to emphasize my ire.

“Don’t go, Bill,” she shouted back and then walked up to me. Lightning flashed again, highlighting her frame and giving her the appearance of a beautiful siren, preparing to lure me to my doom on the jagged rocks of destiny. "I think I believe you."

"You think?" I retorted. Behind me, I heard Tovey's Land Rover start up.

He reversed slowly and rolled to a stop beside us. Another flash and thunder grumbled menacingly above us. He opened his window and spoke to Anne.

"You coming?"

Anne shook her head. "No, Graeme, I want to look into Bill's case a bit more."

"His case?" cried Tovey incredulously. "The only case he's had recently is a case of whisky. Come on, Anne, get in." "Go home, Graeme. I'll call you."

I could hear his teeth grating even above the rumbling of the omni-present storm. "Don't bother. You're as nutty as he is."

"Get stuffed, Tovey," I growled. "By the way, expect a nice letter from my solicitor and a bill for the damage to my car."

"You said you forgave me. You wouldn't..."

"Try me," I threatened. I must say that there is something to be said for this kind of aggressive verbal banter. I made a mental note to thank the Men-In-Black when I saw them next—if I lived long enough, that is. Tovey muttered something under his breath and drove off into the tempest.

I unlocked my passenger door and opened it so that Anne could climb in. I then jogged around the car and got in the driver's side.

As I sat and fired up the engine, I glanced across at Anne, who smiled at me shyly.

"Your place or mine?" she asked coyly. I raised a soggy eyebrow.

"I think that yours is probably the safest bet. I know that my house is definitely bugged. Yours might not be—I know how to check."

"You're telling the truth, aren't you, Bill." She looked at me, those huge eyes causing a shiver to tremble down the entire length of my body. I had not been this close to her since the divorce and my hormones were going haywire. Down boy! "What do you mean, you can check to see if the house is bugged? Have you been taking secret agent lessons?"

"Trust me. I'm Lewis, Bill Lewis," I said in my best, bad, Sean Connery accent.

I drove the short distance to Anne's house; the same place where we had both lived during unhappier times. As I pulled into the short, gravel driveway, I expected to see Tovey's monster parked there, but it was nowhere in sight.

The rain still lashed the windscreen, so I let Anne get out first to unlock her front door. Who said chivalry was dead?. I eased out and quickly scanned the area for black cars and/or pinstriped zombies. Satisfied that no visual surveillance was evident, I rushed across to Anne in the porch. The security light illuminated her from above and glistened off her dripping hair making her look quite, er, wet.

We entered the house and walked down the hall to the living room. As Anne closed the front door behind me, I turned on the main light in the lounge and sat down awkwardly on the edge of the couch. It was a very peculiar feeling. I had lived there for years, but now I felt like a total stranger intruding on Anne's personal territory. I supposed that I was.

I heard her go upstairs and then come back down a few seconds later. She entered the living room and handed me a clean, white towel. It had been my towel once upon a time and had the initials BL embroidered into one corner. I began rubbing my scalp and when I surfaced for air, found that Anne had extinguished the main light and had turned on the standard lamp in the corner of the room, its soft radiance casting delicate shadows around the furniture. I felt my hormones surge again and it took a great effort of will to force them back into submission.

When she had finished towelling her hair, Anne took my soggy linen, went out of the door and into the kitchen.

"Coffee?" she called as I heard her filling the kettle.

"Yes, please. Black, no sugar."

"I know."

While she was out of the room, I took the opportunity to check her telephone. I picked it up and dialled my own number. I let it ring for a while, but heard no ominous clicks. Gratified that my swarthy watchdogs had seen fit to spare Anne, I cradled the receiver and sat back down, after removing my thoroughly moistened jacket. I took it out into the hall and hung it over the radiator at the foot of the stairs.

I joined Anne in the kitchen and watched as she poured steaming water into two large mugs. She stirred her coffee and handed me mine, unagitated.

"So, what do you want to do now?" I asked a little suggestively.

My pheromones must not be very powerful because she seemed not to notice my saucy tone. Damn my submissive hormones! "I'll just get my report forms and then we can sit down and go through your experience one step at a time." She brushed past me and went back into the living room.

"Great," I muttered. Back to bed, boys, your services will no longer be required. I took a sip of coffee to strengthen my shaky resolve and followed her next door. I set down my mug on the dust-free coffee table and sat on the spotless sofa. Anne was standing in front of an immaculately arranged bookcase filled with dozens of neatly marked ring binders. She pulled one out and brought it over to the coffee table, opened it and plonked it down in front of her. Delicately opening the stiff, spring-loaded jaws, she fished out a wad of forms, snapped the jaws shut and placed the binder on the floor by her now shoeless feet. She spread out the papers on the table and took a pen from the tidy holder on thc glass top.

"Okay," she said and plucked the lid from the pen with her teeth. "I'll ask you some standard questions first and then we'll fill out a complete statement."

"Can't wait," I replied sarcastically and took out my cigarettes. "Do you have an ashtray?"

"No, I threw them all out." She sniffed the air suddenly. " Can you smell gas?"

"Yes," I answered and stood up to go into the kitchen. "I'll check the cooker." I walked into the other room and inspected the controls on Anne's gas stove. All of them were off.

The smell seemed to be getting stronger. I opened the back door in an attempt to disperse the gas, but the acrid odour just got worse no matter how hard I wafted the air with the door.

Suddenly, I heard the sound of the living room window shattering, followed by a piercing scream.

I rushed back into the lounge and saw Anne, standing in the corner of the room, staring and pointing at a small canister that now lay, surrounded by broken glass, on the carpet. Grey smoke was pouring from one end of the container.

I grabbed Anne and dragged her out of the living room, through the kitchen and out of the back door.

As we galloped across the back lawn away from the house, we heard another noise. It sounded like an incredibly deep gunshot and half a second later, the house exploded behind us, throwing both of us to the ground and the sudden change in air pressure knocking the breath from our bodies.

I struggled to my feet and began to instantly brush searing debris from my clothes. I saw Anne lying on the grass, apparently unscathed, but sobbing uncontrollably. As I watched the house burn fiercely, I heard a car engine start and the screech of wheels as it tore down the road. I helped Anne to her feet and she buried her face in my chest, still crying in painful, racking sobs. We stood there, watching grim-faced as the pouring rain rapidly brought the conflagration under control. A couple of minutes later, distant, wailing sirens could be heard; somebody must have called the Fire Brigade. Several of Anne's neighbours came rushing out to see if we were all right.

The unexpected outpouring of human kindness from Anne's friends snapped the tightly wound elastic of my composure and I, too, began crying in fitful exhalations. Anne looked up into my tear-streaked eyes.

"Don't call me paranoid," I sniffed. "But I think someone's just tried to kill us."

CHAPTER SIX

It had taken the Fire Brigade only half an hour to extinguish the flames completely; the torrential rain and a liberal dousing from their hoses soon saw off the red and orange demons which had consumed Anne's house. Soon, an investigative team was able to start picking through the debris in an effort to find the cause of the explosion. Unfortunately, external forces would prevent the true origins of the fire from ever being revealed.

I accepted another cup of tea from Mrs. Atkins, Anne's next-door neighbour. I smiled at her gratefully and she reciprocated, but never made eye contact. She had never liked me, even when Anne and I had been together. She probably thought that I beat Anne or something (you would have thought the same if you had heard some of our arguments!). But my ex-wife had always got on with her like a house on fire (pardon the pun). She asked the paramedic if he would like a cuppa, but he declined graciously and continued to pack his instruments into the shoulder bag he had placed on the kitchen table.

"You both seem okay, Mr. Lewis," he said. "But I think that I should take you to the hospital for a more thorough check-up—just to be on the safe side."

I looked at Anne, who was sitting across the table from me, and cast her a querying glance. She shook her head slightly, the movement almost imperceptible. I agreed with her completely.

"No. If you say that we're all right, then that's good enough for me."

He shook his head and looked me right in the eye. There, Mrs. Atkins, I thought. He hasn't turned to stone.

"I think you're making a mistake, Mr. Lewis," he said sadly. "You're not showing any symptoms, but both of you could be in shock." He turned his gaze on Anne. "You've just suffered a very traumatic experience, you know."

"I'm getting used to it," I replied enigmatically. He got up, tutted to himself and left the house. As he walked out of the door, he sidestepped to allow a burly, young police constable access. "Have they found anything yet, Constable Pickering?" I asked.

"They're still sifting through the wreckage," he replied as he slipped his helmet off, revealing a shock of curly, ginger hair. "But the lead investigator has found a nasty crack in the main gas pipe to the cooker. That's probably where the smell of gas came from, even though the cooker was turned off. The curious thing is that the main source of the fire seems to be in the living room."

"Did they find the canister?" Anne asked shakily.

"I'm sorry, Mrs. Lewis, but the entire room was gutted. Even the floorboards have been totally destroyed; so frankly, I don't believe that any canister will be found."

Anne and I had made a complete statement to PC Pickering earlier and now I was beginning to suspect that he did not entirely believe us.

"You don't believe us do you," I said, expressing my thoughts verbally.

"Well, your story is a little far-fetched, isn't it?" He accepted a hot cup of tea from Mrs. Atkins and thanked her sincerely. "Why would anybody want to have you killed?"

I had not informed him of my own fears, that there was an effort to stop me from telling the tale of my abduction, so I merely shrugged. "I don't know. I was hoping that you could shed some light on it."

"Well, we'll do our best," Pickering said noncommittally. "But I'm sure that the investigators will find that the faulty gas pipe was the cause of the fire. You are a smoker, aren't you?" He looked at the brimming ashtray in front of me.

"Hang on a minute," I fired back. "I didn't have a cigarette before the explosion. Don't you think that if I had, we would have gone up with the house?" He looked at me as though I was a naughty schoolboy trying to lie my way out of a caning. "Oh, forget it!"

Pickering took a gulp from his cup and set it down on the table. "There is some good news." I raised a tired eyebrow at him. "Somehow, your car escaped this episode completely unscathed."

"Great," I said without enthusiasm.

"Aren't you pleased?"

"My wife's house has just gone up in smoke and I'm supposed to be happy that my car is all right?" I lit yet another cigarette and the kindly Mrs. Atkins shot me a reproving glance. Sod off, you old bag, I thought with considerable satisfaction.

"Look, Mr. Lewis, I know you've had a rough time, but I'm only trying to help. There's no point in taking it out on me."

Mrs. Atkins spoke quietly, as if to alleviate the tension building in the room and placed a gentle hand on Anne's shoulder. "You can stop here if you like. I have plenty of room."

A silent exchange passed between Anne and I. "No thanks, Mrs. Atkins. It's very kind of you, but I'll be staying at Bill's."

The hand was quickly withdrawn and an expression of disdain flashed across the old woman's lined face. "Well, all right then. I'm sure you know what's best."

Anne stretched and did a very convincing fake yawn and I took this as my cue to speak. "Is it all right if we go now?" I asked of PC Pickering.

He consulted his notebook and then looked up at me. "I think you've told us all that we need for now. Will you and Mrs. Lewis be staying at your house?"

"Yes," I lied immediately.

"Very well, we'll call you if we find anything further."

I gathered Anne and we hastily exited the house, Anne thanking Mrs. Atkins for her kindness as we tumbled out of the door.

The rain was still coming down in sheets and we were both thoroughly soaked again by the time we got next door. As we passed the front door of Anne's house, I ventured a peek inside.

I was surprised to see that the hallway and the kitchen beyond were surprisingly intact; only a few ugly scorch marks on the walls and blistered paint on the woodwork remained as evidence of the inferno we had barely escaped from.

Then I saw my jacket lying sorrowfully on the floor by the radiator and I realized that my car keys were still in its right hand pocket. I collared a passing fireman and asked if the house was safe to enter. He said that it was, but to stay out of the living room as the investigators were still busy in there. I watched as he waded through two inches of filthy water into the kitchen. I followed him and retrieved my soddened jacket from its watery grave. Turning around to leave, I spied Anne's raincoat hanging on a hook behind what was left of the front door. I grabbed it, amazed to discover that the lining was completely dry and handed it to her as I squelched back outside.

As she slipped it on, I wandered across the muddy lawn and stole a glance through the shattered living room window.

Pickering had been correct—the entire room was gutted. Several men in heavy, black coats were poking around the debris and bagging items of interest. I saw that they were skirting a large, almost perfectly circular hole in the floorboards and as I peered upwards, I saw that part of the living room ceiling had collapsed and a section of the front bedroom had come crashing down into the lounge below. A chest of drawers sitting forlorn and smashed in the corner of the room confirmed my observations. Several pairs of Anne's knickers and a flock of bras were scattered around it as though they had been attempting to escape when the conflagration had consumed them.

I called through the window to the nearest investigator. He looked up from a piece of wood he was holding and acknowledged my hail.

"Doctor Lewis?" he said as he picked his way to the windowsill. I nodded. "Bloody mess, isn't it?"

"Certainly is," I agreed and indicated the yawning chasm behind him. "How do you explain that?" I queried.

He glanced at the hole, then turned back to me, placing the wood on the sill and stuffing his grubby hands into his pockets. "To be truthful, Doctor Lewis, we can't explain it yet." At least he was honest. "This room seems to have been caught by the brunt of the fire, but the ruptured gas main was in the kitchen, which apart from a few blown out windows and peripheral damage is relatively unharmed. I just can't explain it."

I told him of the canister which had come crashing through the window. He eyed me suspiciously, then he shrugged, picked up the piece of timber again and turned it over in his hands.

"I suppose we can't rule anything out at this stage."

"Try telling that to PC Pickering," I said venomously. I saw that one of his comrades had climbed into the shallow hole and was gesturing for the man in front of me to look at something. "I think your friend wants you."

"What?" He turned to the other investigator, who was bending over something in the pit. "Have you found something, Smith?"

"Yes, come and take a look at this." "Can we go now, Bill?" asked Anne from behind me. She had put on her raincoat and was gesturing towards my slightly singed car.

"Just a minute, I think they've found something important." I watched, fascinated, as Smith handed something small and jagged to his superior.

He dropped the artefact into a small, clear plastic bag and brought the package to the window. Anne joined me by the charred frame and swore as a ragged piece of curtain, agitated by the wind, slapped her soggily in the face.

"Any idea what this is?" asked the fireman, holding up the bag in front of us. I took a good, hard look at the relic within.

It was a small, grey piece of plastic, slightly melted around the edges. Its colouring and texture were very similar to that of the canister. I looked at the investigator, twin rays of hope beaming from my eyes and illuminating the room beyond.

"That's it!" I cried. "It's a piece of the canister I told you about."

He opened the bag and sniffed the contents expertly. "I can't smell anything like explosives or fuel," he observed and my rays winked out abruptly. "I'll send it to the lab and maybe they can tell us something. But, I'm telling you now, Doctor Lewis, this could just as easily be part of a TV remote control as far as I'm concerned."

"But..."

"But I'll reserve judgement for now. If it is anything of import, I'll have Constable Pickering contact you."

"I'd prefer it if we could get in touch with you personally."

"That's not procedure." I looked at him pleadingly. "All right," he conceded. "Here's my office phone number—ask for Thompson." He handed me a small, white card with neat typewritten numerals on one side and the words ROGER THOMPSON F.I.S. printed on the other.

"Thanks a lot," I said sincerely and slipped the card into my pocket, wondering if I would live long enough to use it. I turned to Anne, who looked thoroughly miserable in the downpour, and took her hand. "We can go now," I said and led her to the car.

I reversed the car down the drive, steered between two dormant fire engines and drove, relieved, away from Anne's wrecked house.

"So, where are we going?" asked Anne once we were on our way. "Your house?"

"I don't think so," I replied. "They'd obviously have another go at us if we went back there."

"Perhaps they think we're dead already?" she suggested.

"Don't bet on it. They seem to know every move I make. They must have people all over the place, keeping tabs on me." I hit the steering wheel, making Anne jump. "Sorry," I said. "But I don't even know why they, whoever they are, are doing this to us! It's not as if I asked to be scooped up and frightened half to death by shitty little grey things with a penchant for beef."

"So, where are we going?" Anne repeated, hoping the change of subject would calm my severely shattered nerves. It didn't.

"I know just the place to go," I said and gripped the steering wheel more tightly.

CHAPTER SEVEN

Loughfield Observatory was a modest affair of wood and brick, only its dome-shaped, revolving roof was constructed of metal. Located roughly twenty miles south of Stockley and eighty miles north of Waleford, the site was technically a part of the campus of the University of Loughfield—although it was several miles from the main faculty, perched on a lonely hilltop overlooking the town.

The storm had dissipated about halfway along our journey and as we entered the town, stars began to glimmer through the rapidly deteriorating cloud-base. I had the window down and was puffing frantically on a cigarette when the bells of the Loughfield Parish Church pealed the midnight hour, their tolls echoing with alarmingly blatant veracity. Driving cautiously through the deserted streets, I eventually pulled up outside a branch of the Midland Bank.

Telling Anne to wait in the car, I jumped out and inserted my card into the automated cash dispenser set into the front of the building, by the darkened main doors. I tapped in my PIN number and flinched when I was suddenly surrounded by brilliant white light.

I whirled around, my heart pounding like a creditor's fist rapping on the front door of my chest. I breathed a heavy sigh of relief when I saw a red Nova amble by slowly. When its rear lights had disappeared round the corner, I returned my attention to the cash machine (or The Money Spitter, as my mother always called them) and withdrew a hundred pound's worth of crisp tenners. When the robotic teller spat my card back out, I climbed back into the car and headed in the direction of the main university campus.

"I thought you'd stopped smoking again," said Anne as I lit another cigarette.

"You know what thought did," I replied acerbically.

"Where are we going?" she asked, not a bit put out by my joyless wit.

"You'll see." She started to say something, but I raised my index finger to silence her and she closed her mouth glumly. She had never done that when we were married. A couple of years ago, she would have bitten off my finger and chewed vociferously on its throbbing, bloody remains. Maybe she had changed since our break-up, Tovey moulding her into his own comatose image, or perhaps she was still in shock from seeing her house go up in smoke. I favoured the latter theory.

I drove through the town centre, past the parish church, and followed several grimy street signs until the security gate of the university loomed in front of us. I stopped by the guardhouse and smiled with false joviality at the approaching security guard. He smiled back at me from beneath a huge peaked cap that was at least two sizes too big.

"Evening, Doctor Lewis," he said, his thick grey moustache doing the Highland fling as he spoke.

"Hello, Jack. Is it okay if I park the car in the main car park for the night?" I glanced at Anne and winked back at the aged sentry. "We're going to one of the clubs in town and I don't want to be tempted to drive home after a skinful."

"Course you can, Doctor Lewis. Here, I'll raise the barrier for you." He ducked back into the guardhouse and a second later, the heavy red and white bulwark lifted into the air.

I gave Jack a cheery wave as the car rolled into the university grounds and a glance into the rear-view mirror afforded a glimpse of the barrier descending behind us. I parked the Maestro in the nearest available space and we got out, the chilly night air causing us to shiver beneath our damp clothes. Taking Anne's hand, I led her back to the main gate.

"Have a nice night." Jack winked at me from the protective cocoon of his security lodge. As we passed, I could see the nicotine-stained interior of the cabin, its light brown walls obscuring the fact that, when new, it had been painted a brilliant white. No wonder the students called it The Iron Lung. I then thought, with a little guilt, about the state of my own lungs and, after one last drag, flicked my cigarette into the night.

We strolled through the gate and turned left, heading towards a brightly-lit phone box a few hundred yards away. I rummaged through my trouser pockets and was rewarded with a shiny ten pence piece. We reached the telephone box and I pulled open the heavy door. It groaned loudly in the silent street. I stepped inside and Anne squeezed in next to me. Pulling out my wallet, I produced a soggy, yellow card from its moist interior. I dialled the number on the card and listened as a voice with a thick Asian accent spoke into my ear.

"Express Cars," said the disembodied voice.

"Could I have a taxi right away, please?" I asked. The voice responded in the affirmative and asked where I was and enquired as to my destination. "We're at the phone box by the university and we're going to Stockley."

Anne looked at me and raised a querying eyebrow.

The voice said that a car would be dispatched immediately so I thanked him and hung up. We stepped back out onto the pavement and waited for our carriage to arrive.

"Why are we going back to Stockley?" Anne asked, looking up at me as she leaned back against the kiosk.

"We're not," I replied and began to observe the now star-filled sky. "I just want to make sure that we reach our destination in one piece."

"Don't you think you're being just a little over cautious?"

"Excuse me?" I shot back. Anne could be so dense at times, but then again, she did have a degree in sociology from the Open University. "You were there when somebody just tried to blow up your house with you inside, weren't you?"

She shrugged. "I'm sorry. I'm obviously not handling this as well as you."

"Evidently," I replied with a little too much vehemence in my voice. She looked at me, obviously hurt and I regretted my tone. "Look," I apologized. "I'll get us both through this. I promise."

Suddenly a pained expression crossed her face. “Graeme!” she cried. “He was probably seen in the Plough with us. What if they’ve got to him?”

At that precise moment, I could not have given a monkey’s turd for Tovey’s well-being, but I just said, “I’m sure he’ll be all right. He’s not stupid, you know. No matter what I say.”

I was lying through my teeth. The more I thought about it, the more certain I was that Tovey was sprawled in a ditch somewhere with several large bullet holes at key points on his chubby body.

The thing is, I felt strangely detached about Graeme’s fate. The man was not exactly my friend, but nor was he an enemy as such. My cold aloofness troubled me more than I cared to admit. Anne, on the other hand, was obviously extremely worried about him. He was, after all, a close personal friend of hers, even after the coarse remarks in the pub car park. I was pulled from my reverie when the taxi pulled up beside us.

We piled in, a barrage of Indian music assailing our ears.

“Going to Stockley?” the driver asked. “It’ll cost you a fair bit.”

“No, I’ve changed my mind,” I responded. “Take us to the observatory.”

“You’re the boss.” He was obviously miffed at having lost a large fare.

The raucous Bhangra music continued its unabated attack on my eardrums and by the time we had reached Loughfield Observatory and climbed out of the car, my hearing was severely impaired. I paid the driver with one of my new tenners and told him to call it a straight fiver. I barely heard him thank me over the ringing in my ears, took my change and watched as he roared off into the night.

Anne and I appreciated the building in front of us. The large, arced doors on the dome of the observatory were wide open, proving that somebody was present, using the facility's thirty-inch reflector. Had it been any other night, I would have been happy to observe the rings of Saturn or do a spectroscopic analysis of the nebulous gases around the Pleiades. But tonight I just needed a quiet place to hide.

I strode towards the observatory entrance with Anne in tow, pulled open the battered metal door and stepped inside. The great telescope towered above us as we squinted into the pervading gloom.

"Robert?" I called out. There was no answer. I turned to Anne, starlight reflecting from her dark eyes. "He's probably in the control room."

I led her to the far side of the dome and through a door into a dimly-lit office. Several computer disc drives were arranged along one wall, printers and plotters along another and a trio of glowing monitors were nestled on a long bench at the far side of the room. A single, flexible reading lamp cast oblique shadows across the form of a man in front of one of the terminals. He had his feet up on the bench, almost touching the keyboard there, and was slumped back in the chair, snoring cacophonously. On the monitor by his feet a group of faint galaxies were gradually growing more defined as a flashing cursor zipped across the screen.

I crossed the room and bent quietly over the sleeping form. Then, with expert precision, I plucked a large, black hair from his left nostril. His feet crashed to the floor and he sat bolt upright, snorting like a bull rhinoceros. Several seconds of expletives followed and then he looked up to see who had disturbed his valuable slumber. His face turned drip-white.

"Doctor Lewis," he stammered. "I didn't expect it to be you."

"You'll not get your doctorate by sleeping on the job," I smiled.

"Sorry, sir," he spluttered. "But, I was just imaging the Virgo Cluster and must have dozed off."

I gave his shoulder a friendly squeeze. "Don't worry about it, Robert. In fact, I came here for your help."

"My help?" He stared at me incredulously. I was getting a lot of those kinds of looks lately. It must be par for the course when you've been kidnapped by aliens.

"I was hoping that Anne and I could stay here for a few days." I stabbed a thumb over my shoulder and Robert noticed my ex-wife for the first time.

"What, here at the observatory?"

"Well, I was thinking more of the lodge next door."

He mused over this for a while.

Robert had been appointed as caretaker for the observatory whilst he completed his thesis. He had jumped at the chance. In addition to looking after the telescope, building and grounds, he got virtually unlimited access to the imaging equipment and free accommodation in the small cottage next door to the main building. He continued to rub his bristled chin and looked me up and down.

"You two in trouble with the law?" He sounded like some gangster in a cheap detective novel.

"No, nothing like that," I half-truthed. "It's just that we need to keep a low profile for a day or two while we sort something else out."

"Well, who'd have thought it? Doc Lewis the fugitive. Of course you can stay, sir. The place is a bit of a mess, though." "That's the least of our worries," I replied gratefully.

The young student led us out of the observatory building, across a small lawn and through a white gate set in a handsome picket fence. We found ourselves outside a tiny, two-up, two-down cottage; its exterior almost invisible in the black, moonless night. Robert opened the door without unlocking it, ushered us in and turned on the lights.

His remark that it was a bit of a mess was an understatement in the extreme. Untidy piles of computer printout littered the floor, obscuring the faded carpet. Atop virtually every stack was an empty pizza carton and ugly coffee rings adorned every uninhabited surface. I have to admit that I felt a little ashamed because it reminded me of home. I wondered if anything remained of my house, or had that place been reduced to a pile of smouldering rubble like Anne's house had.

"Just clear a space and sit down," said Robert as he weaved his way to the kitchen. "I'll put the kettle on. Tea or coffee?"

"Coffee, please," said Anne lightly. "And I could do with something to eat, if that's all right."

"Me too, on both counts." My eyes passed over the pizza boxes and my hopes of a nourishing meal tumbled out of orbit like an abandoned Russian space station. "Should I order out?" I ventured optimistically.

"No, no, Doctor Lewis. I always keep some food in the house for emergencies." I could hear Robert frantically searching his cupboards. After a while, his head popped around the edge of the door. "Er, the number for the Pizzeria is next to the phone. Mine's a deep-pan seafood with extra anchovies."

Anne and I smiled at each other as I picked up the dusty telephone and dialled the pizza parlour. I ordered Robert's deep pan and decided on a regular ham and pineapple for Anne and me to share.

Robert brought in our coffees and we sat and chatted about astronomical matters until the food arrived. I paid for it and we all munched in silence. Our host lit the gas fire and within minutes we were toasting in its comfortable warmth. Once my pizza had been wolfed down, I belched uncouthly and sparked up a cigarette. Robert handed me an ashtray with his free hand; the other still clutched a succulent slice of his favourite dish.

"You could have waited till the rest of us had finished," scolded Anne, her mouth brimming with ham and cheese.

"Don't talk with your mouth full," I replied and sucked on my filter tip, all the guilt I had felt earlier tucked neatly away at the back of my conscience.

Then I realized that on a previous visit to the cottage, during its tidier days, I had noticed a working shower in the bathroom upstairs. "Can I use the shower?" Robert nodded over the edge of his pizza box; his table manners were obviously more refined than Anne's. I finished the cigarette, excused myself and trotted up the stairs.

"There's a couple of dressing gowns in the wardrobe," Robert called after me. I thanked him and detoured through his bedroom.

It was probably the most satisfying shower that I had ever had in my life. After rolling around in the mud of Anne's back garden, being littered with flaming debris and chilled to the bone by icy rain, I felt as though the steady stream of hot water was washing all of my current troubles down the plughole along with all the grime from my aching body.

After twenty minutes of uninterrupted indulgence, I turned the water off and stepped from the bathtub. I quickly towelled myself dry (it was freezing in the bathroom) and slipped on the robe. I was fastening the belt when I heard a loud rap on the door downstairs. It was a very officious-sounding rap and my heart stopped beating for several seconds while Robert answered it.

I opened the bathroom door a crack and peered down the steps. The front door of the cottage was clearly visible and I could see Robert about to open it. He turned the handle and the door exploded inwards, throwing him across the room. He came to rest, unmoving, at the bottom of the stairs.

Anne began screaming incessantly.

Two figures entered the lodge—two figures in pinstriped suits and black hats. My friends from the motel. I saw one of them pass out of view and I feared the worst when Anne suddenly stopped screaming. The other inspected the inert form of Robert at the foot of the stairs.

"He's all right, just unconscious," I heard him say. I breathed a quiet sigh of relief.

The Man-In-Black looked up the stairs straight at me!

"Come down, Doctor Lewis." His tone was eerily emotionless. "Your wife and friend are unharmed. You have nothing to fear from us." He began to climb the steps.

My creditors began hammering on my chest again. I began sweating profusely and the odour drifted up into my nostrils. So much for the refreshing shower. I dashed over to the tiny window and tried desperately to open it, grunting and spitting like a herd of wildebeest. My fight-or-flight instincts were in full flight mode.

Unfortunately, the window stubbornly refused to budge. Several decades of sloppy painting had sealed the frame more securely than any welder could have hoped to. The door behind me swung open and I turned to face my creepy nemesis.

I felt my left leg go warm when he reached into his jacket and begin to pull something out.

CHAPTER EIGHT

Five minutes later, I was sitting in the living room, handing the MIB his identity card back.

"It's a fake," I declared and gripped Anne's shaking hand tightly.

The cool demeanour of these two men was terrifying. Their icy, calculating manner made one feel as though you were addressing an automaton of some kind, but when I had given him his ID, his hand had been warm and human-like.

"I assure you it isn't a fake, Doctor Lewis." A groan from across the room made us all look in Robert's direction. He sat up and rubbed his head with an unsteady hand. "See? We are not here to harm you in any way."

I remembered his name from the card. "So, Captain O'Donnell, why did you blow up my ex-wife's house?"

"An unfortunate accident," he replied evenly. I had the feeling that he had been trained to fool polygraph tests with the greatest of ease. A bit like politicians are born to do. "We had no knowledge of the damaged gas-pipe. The canister contained only a mild nerve agent. It would have rendered you unconscious for six hours with no ill effects."

"Boll-"

"But, the agent is highly combustible," O'Donnell continued. "It is still in the experimental stage."

"Rubbish!" I countered. "The stuff coming out of that canister was no nerve gas. It was a grenade of some sort. You deliberately tried to kill us!",

"Really, Doctor. Do you think we would actually do something like that?"

"Yes," I replied with total conviction. "If it suited your department's interests."

Robert came staggering across the room, still nursing his aching head. "What the hell do you..."

"Please sit down, Mr. Jones." The captain turned to his accomplice. "Lieutenant Reese, will you please get something cold for Mr. Jones' head?"

The other agent slipped wordlessly into the kitchen and returned with a bag of frozen peas. He handed it to Robert, who accepted it gracelessly and pressed the cold package against the large goose egg that had formed just above his hairline.

"Who the bloody hell are you people?" the student demanded.

"I'm Captain Nigel O'Donnell and this is Lieutenant Martin Reese. I am afraid that you will all have to accompany us to a secured location."

"Are you going to interrogate us?" asked Anne nervously.

"You will be thoroughly debriefed."

"Yeah," said Robert. "Probably with coshes and knuckle-dusters."

The officer smiled, the corners of his mouth barely moving. “Nonsense, Mr. Jones. If you will come with us, please.” He gestured towards the battered, open door.

“We’re not going anywhere with you,” I announced defiantly. “We are private citizens. You have no authority to order us about.”

O’Donnell reached back into his jacket, but this time he extracted a large, wicked-looking pistol. All traces of the smile had gone from his face—not that there had been much of one on there in the first place.

“Could I put some clothes on before we leave?” I said, looking down at my sweat-soaked bathrobe.

“That will not be necessary. You will be given fresh clothing when we reach our destination.”

They marched us at gunpoint to their odd, black automobile and bundled us onto the rear seat. They then climbed into the front and started the engine. It was the quietest car engine that I had ever heard and the smoothest ride that I had ever experienced.

Through the blacked-out windows, I could just about glimpse the odd streetlight whizzing by, but the almost opaque glass obscured all other outside details. God knows how the two government agents could see where they were going—even the windscreen was of the same ebony sheen.

The interior of the car was also incredibly dark and I could scarcely make out the silhouettes of Anne and Robert on the seat beside me. Only faint, green dashboard lighting illuminated the driver and his superior—and then only just. They looked like ghostly figures seen through night-vision goggles. I felt around the door, but could find no handle or window control. I whispered to Robert and he tried his side to no avail. So, we sat there in silence for ninety minutes, only the hum of the engine and the hissing of tyres on tarmac to relieve the boredom.

I decided that I needed the lavatory.

Then I felt the car slowing down—an almost imperceptible reduction in our forward momentum. We stopped, then almost immediately started moving again. A couple of minutes later, the car stopped once more and our abductors got out.

I expected them to open the rear doors for us, but it soon became evident that we were to be left in *situ* for the time being.

Then a faint, red glow filtered through the dark windows accompanied by a high-pitched buzzing sound.

"Probably decontamination," explained Anne, drawing upon her years of experience with conspiracy theories and rumours of secret government complexes housed under our very noses. To our small party, they were theories no more. I wondered, selfishly, how much of my income tax had gone into this place.

The glow began to fade and the buzzing gradually lessened in intensity until we were sitting in silence and darkness again. Then we were almost blinded when devastatingly brilliant light poured through the opening doors. A deep, echoing voice rumbled into the car.

"PLEASE STEP OUT OF THE VEHICLE AND KEEP YOUR HANDS VISIBLE."

Obediently, we climbed out and found ourselves in a large, pinkish room. The only things that were not rose-coloured were the car, the ring of soldiers pointing automatic rifles at us and the glasses that I was not wearing. The voice boomed again.

"FOLLOW THE SERGEANT TO THE HOLDING AREA."

An immensely muscled soldier with sergeant's stripes barrelled up to us and indicated towards a door that was sliding silently open. We fell in step behind him and our armed convoy brought up the rear.

Before we left the pink .room, I took one last look around and tried to see the door where the car had entered, but could find none. Then we were in a bland, beige corridor and the sliding door closed behind us.

We marched in file along dozens of identical passages (or perhaps we were being led up and down the same corridor, there was no way to tell). Eventually, after passing what seemed like hundreds of like portals, we stopped outside a nondescript door. It was obviously unlocked as the sergeant merely turned the handle and it popped open. We were ushered inside and found ourselves in a rather plush set of rooms, made up to resemble a reasonably expensive hotel suite.

The sergeant gave us a quick tour of the suite, showing us the bathroom, toilet, living room and twin bedrooms. He then left us alone in our elegant prison, but failed to lock the door after him. Our captors apparently thought that escape was quite impossible. I tended to agree with them. We could have wandered around the warren of corridors for weeks without finding our way out.

I flopped down onto the luxurious couch in the living room, pulling the dressing gown over my exposed knees. Not that I was ashamed of my patellas; it was simply quite cold in the room. Robert, still carrying his dripping bag of peas, sank into a soft chair opposite me and chucked his thawing compress onto the glass coffee table, sending a copy of Time magazine tumbling to the thickly carpeted floor. Anne sauntered into one of the bedrooms and began riffling through a large closet.

"There are clothes of all sizes in here," she called out. Robert and I joined her as she pulled out several hangers' worth of garments. She frowned. "These are all men's clothes."

"Try the other bedroom," I suggested and she strolled through the connecting door into the adjacent chamber.

Robert and I selected some clothes from our closet and quickly donned them. My student picked jeans and a T-shirt, while I settled for slacks and a plain, white shirt. I also found some socks and shoes in the bottom of the closet and slipped them on. Robert kept his own, shabby sneakers firmly tied to his feet, as though they were his only tangible link to the outside world.

We went back into the living room and found that the peas on the table had been replaced by a tray of sandwiches and a large teapot with three plain, beige cups. It seemed that sickly, off-brown was the colour of the moment at this establishment. I poured weak, beige (!) tea into the trio of cups and Robert voiced his concern that there was no milk or sugar.

"I think that's the least of our worries," I scolded, peering round the room, trying in vain to detect any sign that we were being covertly observed.

I almost choked on my tea when Anne swept into the room wearing an elegant, long, black evening dress. She had tidied up her hair, applied fresh make-up from a supply in the bathroom and, quite frankly, looked like a million dollars.

I felt my semi-dormant hormones surging again and struggled to suppress them once more. Since I had teamed up with my ex-wife, I was expending more energy keeping my primitive urges in check than I was running around trying to stay alive. Robert's jaw connected with his knees and drool began to leak from the corners of his gaping mouth.

"Nice dress," I said coolly. I was not prepared to let her know my true feelings. She was my ex-wife, you know—with the emphasis firmly on the ex.

"Oh, it's just something I threw on," she blushed. "You okay, Robert?"

"Blab blaa ibff blob," he said.

Just then, the door opened and in stepped an officious-looking gentleman in an immaculate Saville Row suit. Anne's spell was immediately broken. He acted as though he had not even seen the vision in black and joined us around the coffee table.

Without invitation, he sat in the other soft chair, his bony knees almost going up his long, angular nose, and regarded us with piercing, grey eyes. Those orbs matched his hair and, although he exuded an air of wizened authority, his face was unexpectedly smooth, with only the faintest hint of crows' feet and almost invisible wrinkles across his high forehead. He smiled at us, apparently noticing Anne for the first time.

"Please, sit down, miss," he said. His voice was incredibly deep. A rich bass baritone that rattled around the inside of your head long after he had finished talking. "I see that you have availed yourself of our well-stocked amenities. A lovely choice, Mrs. Lewis."

Anne sat beside me on the couch, not thanking the man for his flattering remark. He produced a sealed packet of cigarettes and tossed them onto the table.

"I believe you smoke, Doctor Lewis." He indicated the untouched pack. "Please, take them."

"I think I just quit," I hissed. I did not trust this man as far as I could throw a bucket of steam. "Are you in charge here?"

"Not exactly," he replied. He opened the cigarettes, took one out and lit it for himself. He puffed out a thin stream of smoke. I was gasping for a fag, but I wasn't letting this man, my enemy, see any sign of weakness on my part. "I am Donald Quentin-Smythe, the administrator of this facility, but there are people high above me who make the important policy decisions."

"What, like kidnapping people at gunpoint and blowing up there homes?" I protested.

"Something like that."

"Then you admit that your men deliberately tried to kill Anne and me?"

"Unfortunately, yes." The smile still had not vanished. I assumed that it was tattooed on. "You were threatening to become a security risk. Our group is well aware of your ex-wife's tenacity in ferreting out the truth. We could not allow you to expose this organization's work."

"But now?"

"Now, things have changed. Circumstances require that you be kept alive, at least for the time being."

"That makes me feel better," I replied sarcastically.

"Sir Donald Quentin-Smythe?" said Anne, apparently not hearing our conversation. He nodded and emitted another cloud of chemicals. She turned to me. "He's rumoured to be a leading member of the Orion Committee, a secret group investigating UFO sightings and alien abductions."

"It seems that your intelligence sources are top-notch," said Smythe smartly. He turned to me. "I told you she was tenacious, didn't I?"

"Orion is the British equivalent of the American Majestic Twelve Committee," she continued, ignoring the enigmatic figure opposite us. She went on to explain that both Majestic and Orion were super-secret organizations that employed dubious methods to keep the lid on UFO secrets. Ufologists had been trying futilely to get the respective governments to acknowledge the existence of these controversial agencies.

Quentin-Smythe sat in silence, neither confirming nor denying Anne's charges. I decided to throw my hat into the ring.

"Did you kill Biggins?"

"Who?"

"The farmer in Waleford? His animals were mutilated?"

"Oh, yes. Mr. Biggins," replied the government man calmly. "He was threatening to go to the press. He said that he had evidence concerning the death of his cattle." He folded his arms across his chest, the first sign of discomfort I had seen the man exhibit. "That may or may not have been true. We couldn't take the risk."

"So you admit that too?" I asked incredulously. "You murdered an innocent man in cold blood?"

"It was a matter of national security."

"Bullshit!" spat Anne. "It was a matter of your own career security." She leaped to her feet. "You bastards! You'll never get away..."

"Anne! Sit down and shut up," I ordered. She glared at me, then acquiesced. I turned to Smythe. "I suppose you're going to eliminate us as well." It was not a question. Robert's face had drained of colour. "Will we just disappear or shall we be the victims of an unfortunate accident?" I took a sip of tea to soothe my fear-dried mouth.

"Don't be so paranoid, Doctor Lewis," Smythe snapped. "If you fully cooperate with us, you—all of you—will not be harmed."

"What do you mean, cooperate?" asked Robert shakily.

The suit addressed his answer to me. "I want you to tell our people everything about your experience, Doctor Lewis. You are a qualified scientist, so your testimony will be highly plausible." He uncrossed his arms and leaned forward, peering into my face, his unblinking eyes making mine water. "Then, I want you to volunteer to go back aboard one of the alien vessels."

My cup clattered onto the table, a pool of hot tea spreading across its transparent surface.

"You're crazy!" I shouted.

"No, Doctor Lewis. If you do not do as we ask, then you will be the one who will be called crazy." He stood up and started for the door. "Now, you should all rest. Somebody will come for you in the morning. I suggest that you get a few hours sleep."

After what he had just proposed, I did not think that I would be able to sleep for a week.

CHAPTER NINE

Robert and Anne retired to their respective bedchambers, but I remained in the living room, sitting on the disturbingly comfortable couch. Despite the opulence of our surroundings, I knew that this suite of rooms was also our prison. I felt like James Bond in Blofeld's secret lair. All Quentin-Smythe needed was a white cat and the illusion would be complete.

I reclined, the soft cushions folding around me, mentally reviewing recent events and made a glum forecast for the future.

Less than two days ago, I had been a sceptical scientist, doing my best to pooh-pooh the very idea of visits to our planet by extra-terrestrials. Now here I was about to be forced on board one of their ships for a second time. I was of no doubt that if I did not volunteer for the assignment, then Smythe would have all three of us eliminated. Beneath that cultured, polished exterior lurked the heart of an ambitious lunatic—I was certain of that fact.

Sitting upright again, I picked up an empty teacup and slowly turned it over in my hands. Then I leaped to my feet and threw the vessel across the room in a fit of frustrated anger. The cup shattered against the far wall with a satisfying crash.

My options were running out faster than condoms at a nymphomaniac's convention.

Either I went along with Quentin-Smythe's plan and possibly never came back or I refused and we all died. Or we could try to escape.

I mulled over the possibility of fleeing through this labyrinthine facility with its countless, identical corridors and probable hundreds of armed security personnel. Luckily for me, I had a partially eidetic memory. I was certain that it could guide us back to the pink room which housed the Men-In-Black's car, if it was still there. I crossed the room and tried the door. It opened when I turned the handle. Poking my head carefully into the corridor, I scanned up and down the length of the puke-coloured passage. I wondered if the Orion Committee and the Waleford Travel Lodge had the same decorators.

There was no one in sight.

I ducked back inside and tiptoed into the bedrooms, waking Robert and Anne and gesturing for them to dress quickly and follow me. Both of them looked at me quizzically and I mouthed the word 'escape'. Anne nodded, but Robert shook his head frenetically and I had to grab his arm to make him come with us.

We entered the corridor and I followed my mental roadmap to the pink room. We did not see a single living soul during our long, nervous journey. The door slid open dutifully and we stepped inside.

The huge black car squatted in the centre of the chamber, just as we had left it. We hurried over to it and tugged on the door handles. They popped open and we clambered inside. The front seat of the car stretched across from the passenger side to the driver's door, so all three of us fitted snugly in the forward half of the vehicle. I looked around the steering column for the keys or a keyhole, but could find neither. I slammed the steering wheel with the heels of my hands in frustration. Then Anne pointed to a small, red button in the centre of the wheel. I depressed it and was immediately gratified to hear the near-silent engine start up.

Unfortunately, I could not see out of the semi-opaque windows.

Then I saw O'Donnell's black sunglasses perched neatly on the dashboard and a notion struck me. I snatched them up and slipped them over my eyes. Instantly, the black window glass became perfectly transparent.

"Polarised lenses and windows," I explained to my two compatriots. "Very clever."

I shifted the gear stick into reverse and hoped that was the right direction to go. Slamming my foot hard down on the accelerator, the car lurched backwards and raced rearlong towards a very solid-looking pink wall.

Then we were though, the black of night camouflaging our dark getaway car. I looked forward and saw a large, jagged pink blob framed by the immense, black doors of an aircraft hangar. We were on an airbase, I realized. I put the car into gear (it was an automatic) and did an impressive handbrake turn to face the opposite direction.

Suddenly all hell broke loose around us.

Intensely brilliant searchlights winked on, capturing us in their cold glare. I put the pedal to the metal, as they say, and the car screeched forward. A blaring alarm began to sound from the hangar behind us.

I followed the road, weaving the car so that the searchlights had a harder time locking onto us, and hoped that the perimeter gate was in this direction. Above us, I heard the sound of whirring rotor blades, their incessant chatter drowning out the cacophonous alarm.

Soon, my headlights reflected off a small, wooden building beside a huge chain-link gate. Khaki-clad figures rushed out of the structure and lined up between our car and the exit, each of them dropping to one knee as they did so. Almost immediately, stark, strobe light flashes illuminated their silhouettes. They were firing their automatic weapons at us! Anne and Robert slid down into their seats and I slouched down as far as I could. Evil sparks ricocheted off the car's bodywork.

I kept my foot hard on the gas pedal.

The soldiers dove for cover as we roared past and smashed through the mighty gate, shattering the windscreen and sending wicked shards of glass flying over our heads. Wind blew in my face as I peered above the dashboard and the sounds of more gunfire could be heard echoing behind our fleeing vehicle. I snatched the glasses from my face and tossed them out of the window, their polarized lenses now useless. As we raced away, the sounds became more sporadic and when we rounded a wide bend, they ceased altogether.

We had made it!

I told Anne and Robert to stay down, just to be on the safe side and drove the car as fast as I could away from the secret base, gazing nervously into the rapidly lightening sky. I could still hear the hum of rotor blades, but no sign of

a helicopter could be seen. As we exited the bend, it became quite apparent where the helicopter was.
It was hovering barely two feet above the road directly in our path. A gigantic carnivorous insect ready to pounce on its feeble prey.

I thought, *what the hell*, and stubbornly refused to slow down. I drove headlong towards the chattering machine and screamed as we passed directly beneath it. I opened my eyes and saw that we were still alive. Looking into my wing mirror, I smiled as the helicopter soared away into the morning sky.

I was steering the car along a bumpy, pot-holed country lane, mile upon mile of unbroken heathland sped by our bullet-riddled steed. I had no idea that the English countryside could be so big, that anywhere in this green and pleasant land of ours could be so isolated. I was getting used to staggering revelations these days.

"You can get up now," I said to my two prone passengers.

Anne poked her head above the dashboard and shielded her face as the biting wind whistled through the non-existent windscreen. Robert stayed where he was.

"Robert?" Anne gave him a gentle shake. He did not move. Then she noticed the bloodstain on the door. "Oh my god!"

I glanced across, also seeing the crimson smear, and brought the car to a screeching halt. As Anne struggled to pull him up onto the seat, I opened my door and rushed around to the other side of the black vehicle. Pulling open the passenger door, I almost gagged at the sight before me.

Anne had managed to haul Robert into a sitting position, his head flopping to one side. She saw my horrified expression and turned his head towards her. She screamed.

An ugly bullet hole pierced the back of his head and the projectile had exited just below his left eye, taking a large section of his face with it. Rapidly congealing blood dribbled slowly down his devastated cheek and dripped onto his T-shirt, creating hideous Rorschach patterns on the pale cotton.

Anne looked at me, her face drawn and lips quivering. "W-what are we going to do?"

"Help me get him into the back seat," I replied after a few infinite seconds. I was unable to tear my eyes away from the grisly sight and had trouble keeping down the tuna sandwiches I had eaten earlier. Anne made a disgusted face at me, as though touching Robert's corpse would somehow infect her. "Come on," I urged. "You take his feet and I'll carry this end." Images of butcher's carcasses filled my head and I was inwardly ashamed that Robert should so rapidly become a thing of abhorrence to me. He was my friend and now he was dead—murdered.

I reached in and pulled his lifeless form out of the car and Anne followed him through the passenger door, carefully, but unsuccessfully, avoiding the pools of blood that had accumulated on the floor and upholstery. Once outside, she opened the rear door and lifted Robert's feet onto the back seat. Then, with some difficulty, we managed to slide him onto the dark vinyl, his head bobbing gently as I slammed the door shut.

Anne climbed back into the front as I trudged to the back of the car and opened the boot. I found a grubby, old blanket, screwed into a ball behind a toolbox, and took it with me as I got back into the driver's side.

As I sat down, I twisted around and draped the blanket respectfully over Robert's inert body, shielding him from view. Then I put the car back into gear and we continued our rural journey.

Anne was still trembling, her slender fingers knotting themselves in her lap. "What are we going to do with him?" she asked shakily.

"We've got to find a telephone and tell somebody about all of this," I declared.

"But who'd believe us?" she cried, tears beginning to well in her eyes. "The police will think that we killed him."

"Anne, we have a car riddled with bullet holes wearing government plates and an innocent man with a huge wound in his head bleeding all over the back seat. I think that they'll at least listen to us. They'll at least be able to get their ballistics people to prove that we didn't kill him." It was a conceit, but one that Anne needed to hear at that particular moment.

"I'm scared, Bill."

"Me too, love." I squeezed her hand and told her to keep on the lookout for a phone box. In the meantime, I scanned the road ahead, but also kept half an eye looking up for any unmarked, black helicopters. I knew for a fact that Smythe and his hordes would not let us off the hook that easily.

Suddenly a village appeared out of nowhere. One second we had been driving along a deserted country lane, then the next moment, houses began flashing by on either side.

I slowed the car and we chugged through the hamlet's single, barren street. A lonely lamp burned at the far end of the village and beneath it stood a bright red telephone booth. Victory.

A solitary road sign told us that the village was called Cranbourne.

As I pulled up beside the phone box, a battered Nissan pick-up rumbled by, its open rear laden with full milk crates. The driver eyed us suspiciously, our smashed windscreen and dishevelled appearance causing him obvious concern. Thankfully, he did not stop to ask us any questions and I climbed out and pulled open the kiosk's heavy door.

I dialled 999 and asked for the police. Almost immediately a woman's voice spoke into my weary ear.

"Barnhope Police Station. Can I help you?"

"Er, yes," I stuttered and realized that I had no idea how to explain our situation. I decided on the truth and hastily told her our fantastic story. When I had finished, the line was silent for a long moment.

"Is this a joke?" she asked stiffly.

"No, of course it isn't," I said a little too loudly. "Just send a car out and you'll see." I told her the number of the phone box and hung up, not giving her chance to ask any more pointless questions.

I got back into the car and lit a cigarette.

"Well?" said Anne.

"The police are on their way," I replied hopefully. Actually, I was not sure that they would come at all.

After half an hour, we were rewarded with the sight of a solitary patrol car coming up the road towards us. The driver stopped in front of our battered shambles and I got out to greet him. We met halfway and I brought him to the back passenger door, opened it and showed him Robert's body.

He lifted the blanket and stared in disbelief at the blood and puddings underneath. As he lifted his radio to speak into it, the pick-up truck barrelled down the road and screeched to a halt, the milkman leaning out of his window at the same time. He yelled at us, his face beetroot red.

"I don't know what you've done, fella," he jabbered. "But there's a convoy of mean-looking army trucks headed this way and they look like they mean business. I'm outta here." And he roared off into the morning mist.

As the dairyman raced away, the sound of his engine was replaced by a deeper, more menacing rumble. Anne climbed out of the car and joined us in looking back down the road in the direction of the thunder.

Then, three huge, green military wagons appeared out of the mist and sped past. They came to a stop a few yards farther down the road, blocking the entire width of the highway, and dozens of heavily-armed soldiers began pouring from their murky interiors. Three more trucks arrived and created a similar cordon at the opposite end of the village.

"Charlie Tango Three-One to Sierra Oscar. Can you hear me, Kath?" The policeman was fingering the buttons of his walkie-talkie furiously.

"Roger, Sean," came the reply. "Go ahead."

"Kath, I've got a major situation here. Get all available units out here."

Another, male, voice crackled across the airwaves. "Negative, Charlie Tango Three-One. You are to return to Sierra Oscar; the situation is under military jurisdiction."

I looked at the constable, a gamut of emotions playing across my face. He looked back, the same confusion evident in his own features. He pressed his RT button again.

"Sierra Oscar, to whom am I speaking?"

"Charlie Tango Three-One; that is not your concern." The mysterious male voice was starting to sound more threatening. "If you do not remove yourself from the area, you will be subject to severe disciplinary proceedings."

The soldiers had, by this time, effectively sealed off the entire village, heavy, wooden sawhorses erected at each end of the hamlet cutting us off from the outside world. The troops the deployed around us, weapons drawn, and an uneasy tension filled the air. I felt my bowels becoming very loose.

The policeman stared at me. "Sorry, there's nothing I can do." He turned away. "I have a very bad feeling about all this," he muttered as he returned to his patrol car. He started up the engine and drove away, two of the soldiers removing a barrier so that he could exit.

I looked around the village, curtains beginning to twitch in the handful of houses surrounding our surreal standoff. Then an officer stepped forward, raising a bullhorn to his lips. I was only about thirty feet away from him for Christ's sake!

"Please step away from the vehicle," the electronically enhanced voice bellowed. "You are under military arrest."

A front door opened and a man in his dressing gown stepped onto the pavement, bewilderment evident on his tired face.

"Sir, please go back into your home," crackled Major Bullhorn.

Anne looked across the car at me with wide, terror-struck eyes. A sense of enormous regret washed over me. I had dragged her into this whole, ugly mess. I had got Robert killed. And probably Tovey, too. How many more people would die before my selfish, anarchic resistance to authority was satisfied. I felt like a serial killer who had realized the extent of his degradation and had decided to redeem himself before an angry jury. I made a decision. One that would change my life in ways that I could not even have dreamed of.

"I'll come quietly," I called, sounding like a bank robber in some tacky, low-budget thriller. I gestured towards Anne. "If you let her go."

"You will both be taken for questioning," came the thunderous reply, devoid of all emotion. Was there something in government tea that stripped one of all feelings? Pop into your local dole office to see what I mean. "If it is ascertained that the woman is not a risk to security, then she will be released unharmed."

"We have no choice, Anne," I said, gazing into her petrified eyes. I gave her a wan smile and she reciprocated the feeble gesture.

We stepped forward and four soldiers rushed forward, their rifles trained on us belligerently. I gave Anne's hand a reassuring squeeze, as much for my own moral as hers, and we were bundled into the back of one of the trucks.

Before we were whisked away, I saw an army flatbed pass through the cordon and several khaki-clad men began heaving the ruined MIB-mobile onto its exposed back. Goodbye, Robert, I thought.

Major Bullhorn, followed by half a dozen tough-looking infantrymen, climbed into the back of our truck, eyeing us warily. The wagon started up and we roared away from the tiny, astonished village.

"I suppose Sir Donald has something nice in store for us?" I queried. The warriors said nothing, their granite faces staring ahead blankly as if we were not even there. "I thought so."

An hour later, after a frightfully bumpy ride and several demeaning strip-searches, Anne and I were sitting back in the same suite of rooms that we had so daringly escaped from a hundred years ago.

Sir Donald Quentin-Smythe paced up and down in front of us, his usual impeccable façade completely stripped away to reveal a new, almost terrifying side to his personality. I suppose I had been right about his dual nature.

"You are both idiots!" he raged, continuing his frantic pacing as he spoke. "Why did you have to run away from us? My god, Mr. Jones is dead thanks to your thoughtless actions."

"Well, what did you expect us to do?" I screamed back at him, my patience with this pencil-necked dickhead wearing very thin. "You held us here against our will. We don't know what you've got in store for us. You as much as threatened to kill us if we didn't cooperate with you."

Smythe held up his hands, stymied by my outburst. "All right, Doctor Lewis. Maybe I did go a little over the top."

"A little?" I shrieked. "Don't blame me for Robert's death. He was killed, murdered, by men acting on your orders." I felt the remorse over my actions beginning to be purged from my system as I continued my verbal assault on the ministry man before me. "If it wasn't for the heavy-handed tactics of your operatives and the intimidating manner in which you present yourselves, then maybe I would have come to you peacefully in the first instance.

"But, no. You had to come on all Do as we say or die didn't you? As far as I'm concerned, you're all murderers. And poor Anne here. She gets dragged into all of this just because I went to her for help. I didn't want to go to the press about my encounter. No. I just wanted help in understanding what had happened to me. But, she still got her house blown up didn't she?

"And don't forget Robert. All he did was to take us in when we needed help. He's dead now, isn't he? I'll bet Graeme is too."

Quentin-Smythe blinked at me, obviously surprised by my heart-felt tirade. He put his hands into his pockets and studied the shiny surfaces of his Gucci shoes.

"I can assure you that Mr. Tovey is very much alive," he stated quietly.

"Well, at least that's one piece of good news," I spat, ready to instigate another attack on him.

Smythe walked across to the door and opened it. "In fact, you could say that Doctor Tovey has been invaluable to us."

He stepped back as another figure entered the room. Anne stood up, surprise etched into her delicate features. I was just stunned.

Wearing a suit as exquisitely tailored as Sir Donald's stood the smiling form of Graeme Tovey.

CHAPTER TEN

"Graeme!" Anne rushed to the newcomer and threw her arms around him. "We thought that you were dead."

"Anne," I said, beginning to understand the situation more clearly. "I don't think that he's a prisoner here."

She stepped back and stared at Tovey, confusion causing her facial muscles to perform acrobatics.

"Sorry, Anne," he said calmly. Obviously, Tovey was drinking the same tea as everybody else around here.

"Yes," interjected Sir Donald Quentin-Smythe. "Doctor Tovey has been one of our finest undercover operatives for some time now."

Anne stared at Tovey in disbelief. "But you've been an active member of our group for ages. You've uncovered untold hundreds of secret documents pertaining to the UFO cover-up. That was your particular area of expertise."

"I was acting under orders. How else would I get my hands on authentic government papers if I didn't already work for them?" There was a hint of smug satisfaction creeping into his voice. "Most, but not all I might add, of the so-called secrets I uncovered were simply disinformation and elaborate cover stories designed to whet your appetites."

"You see," continued Smythe. "We found that the best way to keep a lid on Her Majesty's Government's involvement in the UFO phenomena was to plant operatives deep inside leading ufology research groups. C.O.C.K.U.P. was the exception—we actually set that group up from the outset.

"You see, every government department has its leaks. But if our leaks could be channelled through loony fringe groups and struggling, disaffected scientists," he glanced at me and I stuck two fingers up at him," then the general public would not take them as seriously as if, say, The Times was to publish the MJ-12 documents."

During Smythe's frank admissions, Anne had stared icily at Tovey, unnerving him with her caustic glare. I'm telling you, she could have polished the mirror of my telescope with that look. Then, to everybody's surprise (not least Tovey's) she swung her fist and planted it firmly on Graeme's lower jaw.

"Bastard!" she screamed as he was sent spinning back into the doorway.

He caught himself on the jamb and attempted, feebly, to regain his composure. I goggled at Anne, a new admiration for her filling my chest.

"Anne, I understand that you're upset," said Tovey shakily, his eyes becoming a little watery—ha ha. "But you have to believe that I didn't want anyone to get hurt."

"That's why you told your zombie friends where I lived?"

"But..."

"They destroyed my house, you shithead!"

"It wasn't supposed to happen like that."

She started towards him again, her fists balled, but I grabbed her arm to restrain her. She spun around and shot poison-tipped daggers from her eyes.

"All right, let's all calm down," said Smythe, attempting to diffuse the situation. "Everybody sit down."

I led Anne to the couch and virtually had to force her to sit. I plonked down beside her, keeping a tight grip on her right hand, as much for my own peace of mind as for anybody else's protection. Sir Donald sat in one of the soft chairs and, when he was certain that my ex-wife was not going to rip out his eyeballs and throttle him with his own optic nerves, Tovey sat in the other.

"Now then, Doctor Lewis. I will repeat my request of you." Smythe sat forward, his hands wringing fervently in front of him. "We want you to go back on board one of the alien ships." I started to speak, but he raised a hand and continued. "But, before you ask, we have every intention of bringing you back safely. You will be on, what's the phrase? A reconnaissance mission?"

"Go on," I urged when he paused for a few seconds. I was both fascinated and soiling my pants at the same time. "How can you guarantee my safety?"

Smythe gave Tovey an 'it's over to you' look. "We know that we can bring down one of their ships," said Graeme with an air of confident authority. "And we have several in our possession." Anne issued an expletive centred on the reproduction of several species of unpleasant invertebrates. Tovey continued unperturbed. "But, our process seems to shut down their power supply and, so far, we have been unable to reactivate any of the vessels."

"What about the Americans?" ventured Anne. "I thought that a large part of their stealth programme and the

Strategic Defence Initiative were developed off the back of captured alien technology?"

"We have learned a great deal from our acquisitions," said Smythe. He used the 'we' to imply, successfully, that the American and British organizations were closely linked, if not simply parts of a greater, more sinister whole. "But, their energy source is something of a mystery to us. Graeme."

"We need someone to go aboard one of their ships and gather data on its operational characteristics." He began studying the palms of his hands intently. "Before we shoot it down."

"Someone means me, doesn't it?" I figured. "You're going to blow the ship out of the sky with me still on board?"

The smiles on the two smug faces across the table from me confirmed my nightmare scenario.

"Call me daft," said Anne, raising her index finger, "but how can you assure Bill's safety when you start bouncing artillery shells of the UFO's hull?"

"Don't worry, Mrs. Lewis," smarmed Quentin-Smythe. "Our methods are quite safe."

"Cryptic and totally unreassuring. Quite what I've come to expect." She flopped back into the cushions and sighed deeply. I gave her sweaty hand a gentle squeeze and she smiled flatly in an unconvincing attempt at morale boosting.

Just then, a thought struck me and I told them of my fears. While on the examination table aboard the alien ship, I had been completely paralysed; unable to move a muscle. How was I supposed to get any information when I was flat on my back with my entrails hanging out in front of me?

Anne's face paled as I recounted my traumatic experience of only a couple of days ago.

"We know a great deal about the abduction techniques of the Greys," replied Tovey matter-of-factly. "For instance, we know that they use hypersonic and hypervisual pulses to confuse the nerve impulses to and from the brain. We believe that this is what causes the paralysis felt by so many abductees. Our scientists managed to recreate this technique in the lab and we feel that we can overcome its effects.

"But there is a risk, Bill," Tovey looked me in the eye and I felt a certain discomfort when he used my forename. "You will have to get away from the initial examination area undetected and get all the data within thirty minutes."

"Why thirty minutes?" I asked, feeling my teeth begin to chatter of their own volition. Smythe and Tovey exchanged uneasy glances.

"Because," began Anne's ex-colleague, "half an hour after your insertion, the ship will be hit by a massive electro-magnetic pulse. All its power will fail and it will crash."

"How do I get off the ship before it crashes?"

"Er, you don't," Smythe admitted. Then he added, as if to bolster my fragile hopes, "But if you do find a way to escape before the EMP hits, then by all means use it."

"Gee, thanks," I gasped. "So, you can't guarantee my safety after all?"

"Not exactly," said Tovey. "But in all the thirty-plus crash/retrievals that I have been involved with, only two Greys have been killed as a result of the physical impact." He smiled unappetisingly. "So you see, the odds of you coming back in one piece are really quite good."

"Why can't you send someone trained for this kind of thing?" I pleaded, trying to weasel my way out of a terrifying demise. "Like Rambo? I'll bet Captain O'Donnell would jump at the chance."

"No doubt he would," agreed Smythe. "But these aliens are very discriminating. They do not just abduct anybody, you know."

"Could've fooled me," I grumbled and thought about the apparent randomness of my experience. It could have been anybody on that dark, country lane.

"Oh no, Doctor Lewis. They are very choosy about whom they let on board their ships. But, the chances are that if you've been abducted once, then they'll grab you again. It's happened before."

"Repeaters," muttered Anne, referring to people who had succumbed to multiple abductions, often spread across many years and beginning during childhood. I may have been a sceptic, but I did my homework.

"Exactly," agreed Tovey. He smiled at Anne, but she did not reciprocate.

"How are you going to get him on the saucer in the first place?" I sensed that Anne had developed a very low opinion of these two men over the preceding minutes. "Do you just dial 555-GREY, say you're ready to have your internal organs removed and they come running?"

"Not exactly, miss," smiled Quentin-Smythe.

"That's Mrs. Lewis," she corrected and I was warmed when she gave my left hand a comforting squeeze. Lately, all Anne and I seemed to do was squeeze each other's hands! Not that I was complaining.

"Apologies Mrs. Lewis," he smarmed. "But if you allow me to explain?" Anne nodded wordlessly and Smythe continued. "Contrary to popular belief, we can track the alien vessels on sophisticated radar and, believe me, there are a lot of them whizzing around up there. They are particularly fond of certain locations. Like the area around Waleford, for instance.

"Now, we can place you, Doctor Lewis, near to one of these sites and, hopefully, after a short wait, they will fall into our trap and compliantly pick you up. You will be fitted with an array of recording devices, so you will simply have to walk through the ship and everything that you see will be relayed back to us on the ground."

"I don't suppose I have a choice, do I?" I asked morosely.

"Not really. If you want to rid our planet of these parasites, and believe me, they are parasites, then this will help us forward considerably."

I had a sudden flash of insight—as though a distant memory had become unlocked and had raced into my conscious mind. "To them we are the parasites," I said cryptically. "They were here first and we stole their planet from them." Something else filtered into my waking memory, but I did not vocalize the thought. I could tell from the expression on Anne's face that she knew I was holding something back.

Smythe and Tovey looked at me incredulously, their lower jaws hanging limply around their waists.

"How can you know that?" asked Tovey

"I'm not sure," I admitted. "But when the Grey on the ship spoke to me with its mind, I got all these other images as well. I guess talking about them brought it back out."

"Are you saying that they are natives of the Earth?" asked Smythe, wonderment in his words. "And now they want it back?"

"No," I replied. "They don't want it back—we've spoiled it for them. But, they want to find out what happened in their absence. I—I..." The vision faded and my mouth opened and closed without any issue. “Sorry, it’s gone. Look, I’m absolutely petrified, but I’ll do it. I’ll go.”

“Bill, are you sure?” Anne took my face in her hands and our eyes transmitted a silent, intimate message.

“Yes, I’m sure,” I said eventually. “I’m the only one who can do this.” Then a smile curled my lips. “Plus, I want to get my own back for what they did to me.

“To see their ugly, grey faces as their ship drops from the sky like a brick.”

CHAPTER ELEVEN

There is one thing to say about abject terror—it focuses the mind. The next seven days were the most frantic that I had ever experienced. After dozens of debriefings, recounting my abduction experience to scores of white-coated eggheads time and time again, and what seemed like hundreds of medical examinations, I was declared fit to proceed with my assignment.

Anne remained by my side, stoically offering support when I lapsed into moments of terrified despair. She had been given the opportunity to leave (as long as she signed The Official Secrets Act before she went), but had chosen to stay with me. I had little chance to explore the ramifications of her decision, but as events unfolded beneath our feet, we would become closer than we had ever been. Even more so than when we had been married.

After the interrogations and medicals had been completed, we were transported to the injection site in a convoy of plain, white articulated trucks. The lack of windows in the air-conditioned trailer prohibited me from learning of our destination until the large rear doors opened and I was allowed to step outside.

The air was chilly and rain had transformed the ground into a grey-brown morass. I cast my eyes skyward, and at that moment, the sun peaked from between the clouds. I took it as a good omen and hoped that the suddenly fine weather held out.

As I strolled down the wide ramp at the back of the trailer, I recognized the place immediately. It was the Biggins' farm near Waleford; the site of the murder of an innocent man by Smythe's sinister agents. I felt my stomach muscles tighten as I stepped into the mud of the farmyard to be greeted by O'Donnell and Reese. So much for the good omen.

"Morning, Lewis," said O'Donnell, deliberately omitting my hard-earned title. Now that I was a member of the Orion group, albeit under duress, he felt that I could be treated with the contempt that I deserved. "We have been assigned as your protection for the duration of your stay here," he reported with obvious distaste.

"I feel safer already," I replied sarcastically.

"Look, I don't like this assignment any more than you do, but we both have orders to follow. So let's get on with it." He stabbed his thumb over his shoulder. "I'll show you and your wife to your rooms."

He led us across the farmyard, past groups of feverishly active workers, all furiously setting up hordes of technical equipment, and into the main farmhouse. Reese brought up the rear.

Smythe and Tovey were nowhere in sight. I presumed that they were cooped up, safe and sound, back at the secret airbase.

O'Donnell showed us the kitchen, an ancient, iron range dominating the small room, and then led us down a short, musty hallway to the living room. Everywhere, technicians were fitting sensors to the walls and ceilings, apparently undistracted by our presence.

"Where did you kill the farmer?" I asked conspiratorially. The captain ignored me and took us upstairs to the bedrooms. "Where is Biggins' family?"

"They've been relocated," came the terse reply. He pushed open a door to reveal a small, tidy bedroom. "This is your room, Mrs. Lewis."

Anne stepped inside and gave the chamber a quick once-over. "Very nice," she remarked, testing the springs on the single bed. "I'm glad I haven't any cats to swing about."

O'Donnell smiled grimly and showed me my quarters. It was the room next door and was considerably larger than Anne's cupboard.

"Don't worry," I called to the next room. "You can do all your cat swinging in here."

Anne raced in and surveyed my billet with enthusiasm. She paid particular attention to the double bed, its brass ends glittering invitingly in the light that filtered through the large, open window.

"This is more like it," she grinned. "We'll be very comfortable in here, Captain O'Donnell."

A surge of lustful excitement set my nerve-endings tingling. Unfortunately, our muscle-bound gooseberry was less turned on by the idea.

"Sorry, I am under strict orders that you sleep in separate rooms."

"Bloody Smythe," I cursed. "He's only jealous."

Unexpectedly, O'Donnell smiled, a wide, knowing smile that made him look infinitely more likeable.

"Have you ever seen Mrs. Quentin-Smythe?" I shook my head. "If you had, then you'd be the one who was jealous." He did a hilarious impersonation of a lovesick dog and I found myself roaring with laughter with the two agents. Even Anne joined in and for the first time in days I did not feel as though my world was about to end.

After that, we got on famously with our two escorts and learned all sorts of surprising things about each other. I never let myself forget Biggins' fate at the hands of these two men, though.

We returned to the kitchen and Anne started to prepare a pot of coffee. The technicians had disappeared, their tasks complete, and we were alone in the house. There was still a hive of activity outside, of course, as the Orion techs set up their monitoring stations and the huge EMP gun, which required a whole semi-trailer to house it and another to power the phenomenal weapon. It resembled a small radio telescope set onto the end of a long, octagonal tube. A myriad of pipes and cables clung to the sides of the device and I'd never seen so many men holding spanners in my life.

We sat around the huge, oak kitchen table, sipping Anne's strong coffee and exchanging stories from our pasts. For instance, I was surprised to learn that both O'Donnell and Reese were married with kids (not to each other, of course) and that Reese's hobby was philately. I had difficulty picturing this huge, blond Titan giggling with excitement as he acquired a penny black or a rare first-day cover from the isle of St. Vincent.

Anne was also surprised, and a little frightened, to learn that they had been assigned to follow her for two weeks some six months previously. She explained to me that she had been investigating a mysterious crash in Derbyshire. The locals swore that they saw some sort of brightly-lit aircraft going down in the Peak District, but the Civil Aviation Authority and local air traffic controllers insisted that no aircraft, civilian or military, had been reported missing. Unfortunately for Anne, neither O'Donnell nor Reese could explain the enigma. Apparently it was as much of a mystery to the Orion Committee as it was to everybody else.

I myself had them snorting their coffee when I told them of the time, during a drunken binge, that a gang of my students had stripped me naked, tied a notice around my neck which read: 'IF YOU WANT A BIG BANG HERE'S YOUR MAN' and chained me inside a telephone box in the centre of Loughfield. It had taken ten firemen nearly an hour to cut me out. I got fined a hundred pounds at the magistrate's court for that debacle.

After a light lunch later in the day, O'Donnell gave Anne and I permission to go for a walk in the countryside, as long as we did not go too far. He took the added precaution of handing me a walkie-talkie and instructions to report in every fifteen minutes. I said that I would and we set off, heading out of the gate at the back of the farmhouse and towards a large copse nearby.

The sun had cleared the sky of clouds, save for a few puffy cumulus which sailed merrily over our heads, and the ground was almost dry—a beautiful day for a walk. I found it inconceivable that any ill could befall me on a day like this. This thought was encouraged a minute later when we entered the trees and out of sight of the farmhouse. Anne grabbed hold of me and kissed me firmly on the lips.

When she had finished, I was somewhat taken aback (not to mention breathless). She smiled up at me and took my hand, gently leading me deeper into the woods.

Soon, we found a small clearing, carpeted with soft, green grass. Anne pulled me down onto the ground and we lay there for a few minutes staring at the abstract cloud patterns drifting overhead, the damp grass a minor irritation. I chewed absently on a particularly long blade of grass, my thoughts a whirl of emotions. I was scared to death about my mission, happy that we were finally getting along with our bodyguards and absolutely elated that Anne and I were enjoying each other's company for the first time in years.

"Why did we have to get divorced?" I asked, turning my head and looking in Anne's perfectly formed ear. She had discarded her Roswell earrings and now wore a simple pair of gold sleepers.

"I don't know, Bill," she breathed. "I guess that we were just unsuited for one another back then."

"What about now?" I probed, hoping that my sudden questions did not blow it.

"Let's just take it steadily. Eh?"

"Good idea," I whispered and kissed her ear gently. She smiled and hummed contentedly.

We both raised ourselves onto one elbow and gazed into each other's eyes, seeing depths of regret covered by a dull surface of anxiety. I tried to kiss her, but she pulled her head back, still smiling.

"I thought we were taking it steady?" she said huskily.

"The hell with it," I growled back. I kissed her and this time she did not withdraw.

As we embraced, I felt more content and secure than I had since our initial break up. I could have stayed in this green womb forever. We explored each other, like a young couple that were on their first romantic encounter and it felt wonderful. My heart was gliding, soaring, swooping and any other synonyms that came to mind. Then our raptures were shattered.

"Lewis, are you there?" It was O'Donnell on the walkie-talkie.

I tried to ignore it, as did Anne, but the captain was very persistent.

"Bill, answer me. Over."

I unclipped the device from my belt hook and clicked the RT button. "What is it, Captain?"

"I thought I told you to report in every fifteen minutes."

"Sorry, we must have lost track of the time."

"Well get your arses back here. Control has picked up something heading this way at Mach five. It could be showtime, Doctor."

"But it's the middle of the day! I thought they only came at night."

"Don't be so naive and shuffle your bums back here. On the double."

"Yessir," I snapped and turned to Anne. The frightened look had returned to her beautiful eyes. "Come on, we've got to go."

We rushed back to the farmhouse and found everybody running around in a state of agitated excitement. Our two minders came bursting out of the house as we approached and hurried us to one of the waiting trailers.

"We haven't much time," explained O'Donnell. "They'll be overhead in five minutes." He handed me my uniform.

It was a plain, blue outfit of synthetic fibres. I had been fully briefed in its operation and slipped it on expertly. The one-piece garment was fitted with dozens of recording devices and radio transmitters. The tiny digital cameras and audio recorders were powered by a large, flat battery that was attached to a buckle on my left side. On the right side of the jumpsuit, a special, sewn-in holster had been added and in this nestled a small pistol. I had objected to its inclusion, but Smythe had insisted that it was a necessary piece of equipment and that I was to use it if I felt my life to be threatened. A half a day of firing range training had followed and, not to sound like I'm blowing my own trumpet, I had become quite a good shot. Whether I could shoot at a living target remained to be seen. The gun held ten rounds in a clip that slotted into the handgrip and a spare cartridge was stitched into the lining of the suit. To access it, all I had to do was pull apart a carefully prepared seam and the clip would pop out, ready for use.

Once the suit was on and the battery connected, I turned slowly around inside the trailer. O'Donnell spoke into his radio and then gave me the thumbs-up.

"They're receiving sound and pictures in the other trailer," he explained. "Medical telemetry is also being received from the epidermal sensors in the suit. Here, put these in now." He handed me two small, yellow objects that resembled earplugs. "They're ear-plugs. Specially designed to counteract the alien hypersonic pulse. They're also equipped with tiny speakers so we can speak to you on the radio. Just pressing your finger against the plug activates the mechanism. Now these." He handed me a small, plastic container. I popped it open. Inside were two black discs and a tiny bottle of fluid.

"Contact lenses?" O'Donnell nodded. "To negate the hypervisual pulse?" He nodded again. "Do they hurt?" He shrugged. "Thanks for the confidence boost. I can't do this. Anne, could you put them in for me?"

I handed her the container and she extracted the bottle. She applied two drops of liquid into each of my eyes, then gently inserted the lenses over my pupils, my irises covered by the black discs.

I blinked and looked forward.

"Can you see?" asked Anne curiously.

"Perfectly," I replied, amazed. Even though the lenses were jet black on one side, their concave surfaces were totally transparent. O'Donnell explained that they were manufactured using similar method as the windows in the MIB-mobile. I only hoped that they did their job. I did not relish examining my intestines again.

A voice came over the intercom. "Three minutes," it said. "Speed dropping to subsonic. Waleford ATC has it on their scopes."

"Okay, Reese. Take him to his position," ordered the captain.

The lieutenant gently took my arm and led me from the trailer.

"Good luck, Bill," called Anne and I gave her a cheery wave as I descended the ramp.

I followed Reese across the farmyard and into the cornfield beyond.

"Check RT," he said as I walked into position among the ploughed ruts.

"No chance of a corn circle?" I asked, observing the barren field around me.

"That's a load of crap," replied Reese knowingly. "Check RT, we haven't much time."

"Control, this is Lewis. Can you hear me?" I said, pressing my index finger to my ear and activating the micro-switch inside the earplug.

"Affirmative, Lewis. You are coming through loud and clear. Activate your hypersonic countermeasures now," came the reply.

I pressed the button that Captain O'Donnell had shown me on the battery box and a high-pitched tone filled both my ears. I squinted in pain for a second and then the tone altered and became a lower, more bearable hiss.

"Can you still hear us, Lewis?"

"Roger, Control. You're still coming through. You could've warned me about that god-awful noise, though."

"We wouldn't want to spoil your fun. One minute, Lewis. Get ready." I watched Reese retreat back to the safety of the Control trailer, then my disembodied companion spoke again. "If you look to the north, you should see them coming."

I gazed northwards, but all I could see was the wall of trees bordering the road to Waleford. Nearer the farm, they ended abruptly to be replaced by a dry-stone wall, but no traffic could be seen using the highway. The Orion Committee had seen to it that an accident' had occurred and that a long section of the road had been closed off to normal traffic. They did not want Joe Public witnessing my heroics.

Then I saw it.

Rocketing towards me and growing larger by the nanosecond was a tremendous black triangle, its equilateral form distorted by the distance and perspective. How could anybody not notice that thing tearing across the sky? I thought to myself. You could see it clearly for miles around.

I could not perceive if it was the same vehicle that had snatched me away the previous week—it looked completely different in the glaring sunlight—but it did appear to be about the same size. I stood, absolutely petrified, as the sleek, midnight shape came to an abrupt halt directly above me. The voice spoke into my ear in hushed tones.

"It's exactly one thousand feet over your position. Do not move."

I could not have moved even if I had tried. I was rooted to the spot, an unsavoury smell drifting around me, as the impossibly perfect polygon slowly began to descend. My whispering friend counted out the altitude of the craft as I watched, helpless.

When it had reached a hundred feet above me, it stopped and I had no difficulty estimating the vast size of the alien monstrosity. It was roughly three hundred feet on each of its three sides. Large, grey circles were in evidence at each corner—obviously the source of the blinding white lights that I had seen during my nighttime encounter. Perfectly central of the craft was another, larger circle, but this one glowed faintly; a soft, amber pulsation that was almost hypnotic with its regularity. The body of the ship itself was totally black, with no signs of any external features or seams.

"We are detecting elevated hypersonic and hypervisual emissions from the vessel. Prepare for transport." I did not share my invisible friend's enthusiasm.

Then I was surrounded by the familiar amber glow, its delicate touch caressing my quivering face. I faintly heard the screech of brakes from somewhere in the distance and imagined dozens of armed soldiers converging on the car of a hapless traveller who had somehow managed to elude the roadblocks and stumbled upon this highly sensitive scene. I closed my eyes and waited for the inevitable tingling.

It came and went and, when I opened my eyes again, I found myself in the perfectly white room, lying on the table, naked and sweating. There was no sign of my alien captors and I wondered if the transport process automatically removed one's clothing and deposited one on the examination table. I tested my arms and legs and found that I could move them. So far, so good.

I swung my legs over the side of the table and lowered my feet to the floor. Its surface was surprisingly warm against the soles of my feet. I found my uniform in a crumpled pile on the floor and hastily dressed, checking that all the instruments were still in evidence and working properly. The room was deathly silent. All that I could hear was the hiss of the plugs in my ears.

I whispered to my man in the trailer outside, but could not hear my words in the strange room. To my surprise, I got a reply. My voice was loud and clear over the speakers in the control centre. I was ordered to try and find a door and use it. I had twenty-five minutes before the craft was brought down. It was still hovering above the field, apparently oblivious to the circus of trucks in the neighbouring farmyard.

I looked around the room, seeing the other table and nothing else. No walls, no doors, nothing. I decided to try and find the wall and feel my way round to any portal that might exist. I gaped at the cavernous interior of the room and calculated that it would take several precious minutes to reach what could be the nearest wall.

I took two steps forward and squashed my nose against an unforgiving surface. The room was quite a bit smaller than I had estimated.

The room was so intensely bright that I looked like a mime feeling my way across the wall's frictionless surface. I was about to give up and try another part of the room when I fell forward and tumbled into a dark, steam-filled corridor.

I picked myself up and turned around. I could not see where I had fallen through the wall. All that I could distinguish was a perfectly smooth greyish-blue surface. I reached out my hand and ran my fingers across its veneer. They came away slightly damp.

"Come on, Lewis. This is no time to fart about," admonished my controller.

"Which way do I go?" Suddenly my whisper echoed like a gunshot along the passageway. Sound had returned with a vengeance.

"I don't know! Pick a direction and take it."

I decided to go right and set off at a slow jog. "Are you getting all this?"

"Affirmative. Pictures are crisp and clear."

After a few yards, I happened upon an intersection, where four corridors converged. I headed down the left hand passage, again at a steady jogging pace. Soon, the conduit ahead widened and curved slightly to the right. I loped around the bend smack into one of the alien crewmembers.

The force of my impact sent the small figure sprawling across the floor, but it was immediately back on its feet in a fluid, almost elegant, flurry of spindly limbs. It stared at me with huge, unblinking eyes and I was certain that I saw an expression of recognition cross its wizened face. Could this be the same creature that had smiled at me during my last visit?

I punched it in the face before it had time to remember me too clearly. It fell to the deck, nose slits bleeding and lidless eyes staring blankly at the ceiling just above my head.

Suddenly I heard a shriek. It was a mental wail that set every one of my few remaining brain cells on edge. I whirled around, pulling out the pistol, and came face to face with another Grey, racing down the corridor towards me. It had a small, black rod in its hand and it was pointing straight at me. Without thinking, I took aim with the pistol and released one round at the charging alien.

A spray of bright crimson blood spurted from the bullet hole that had appeared between its bulging eyes. It took three more steps, then fell to the floor, unmoving, beside its unconscious crewmate.

"Way to go, Lewis!" enthused my effervescent friend. He had seen the entire episode on his monitors and I could hear hoots and cheers in the background. I felt sick. In fact, I was sick all down the nearest blue-grey wall. "Aw, Lewis, that's disgusting. And in full colour."

"Well I never killed anyone before!" My shout echoed down the corridor and I clapped my hand to my mouth as though that would stop the already reverberating yell.

"Fifteen minutes, Lewis," he reminded me. "I think there's a chamber ahead of you. We're detecting high-energy readings from that direction. Go that way."

I suppressed another retch and continued my journey into the bowels of the spaceship, leaving the two motionless aliens behind. I stopped in front of a blank wall with no sign of entry. I reached out my hand to touch the dark surface. My shaking appendage passed through the wall with only slight resistance. It was like dunking one's hand into a tub of runny jelly, only not as pleasant. My hand felt decidedly dirty when I extracted it, but there were no stains blemishing my skin.

I took a deep breath and stepped forward, closing my eyes before they reached the viscous material.

I thought that I had stepped outside. All around me was the pleasant countryside surrounding the Biggins' farm. Then, as I looked around more closely, I could see several control stations, each with a small, grey figure sitting in front of it. All of them appeared identical. And naked. It was then that I realized that all of the Greys that I had encountered had been nude. Must be a civilization of voyeurs, I thought. As quietly as I could, I entered deeper into the room, a full, blue sky above my head and green fields on all sides.

Even behind me.

I looked around and saw that what should have been the back wall of the chamber was gone and I could clearly see the farm and all of its outbuildings several hundred feet below me. The Orion Committee trailers seemed disconcertingly tiny from up here.

My mouth was clamped tight shut, but I must have made a mental cry of surprise because one of the Greys turned and looked at me. Its orb-like eyes almost popping out of its head and I heard the beginnings of the psychic shriek again. Its left eye did pop out of its head when my silenced bullet slammed into it.

The other aliens spun round in their seats and saw their comrade lying in a pool of blood on the floor. Well, actually, he seemed to be lying in a pool of blood while floating several hundred feet above the Waleford countryside. In unison, they rose from their chairs and began advancing slowly towards me. I waved the pistol menacingly in front of them and they stopped for a second.

Then a silent message must have passed between them. One that they did not want me to hear. One of the creatures charged at me and I felled it with a single shot.

"Don't come any closer!" I screamed at the child-like figures and brandished the gun again.

Another alien came running towards me and I fired again, sending the monster spinning across the room.

"Control, fire the bloody EMP gun now!" I pleaded.

"We have not acquired the necessary data yet," replied the controller.

"And you're not going to get it either," I wailed. "These buggers are going to tear me apart if you don't do something now."

A third alien raced towards me. I raised the pistol, took aim and squeezed the trigger. Nothing happened. The gun had jammed. I fumbled with the weapon and the alien dove on me. Dropping the firearm, I raised both hands to protect my face as the creature raked at me with its sharp, grey fingernails. I screamed and the controller must have realized that I was in true danger.

The ship lurched to one side and all around us, the scenery vanished as the walls became opaque. I was thrown across the room and I heard an oral squeal of pain from my assailant as my heavier body crushed its frame against the wall. We flopped to the deck and I threw off my savage attacker, surprised that such a fragile creature could display such strength. A single shove sent it flying across the cabin and onto the consoles at the far end. Another squeal and it lay, silent, against one of the stations.

The four remaining aliens were too wound up with their own problems to pay any attention to me as they scrambled back into their seats and tried frantically to get the ship level again. I hoped that my cameras were still transmitting pictures to the trailers as I watched them work the controls furiously. I had been informed at an earlier briefing that the electronics of my equipment were EMP shielded.

The ship lurched again as another burst struck its ebony hull. Briefly, the walls shimmered and the outside world came into view once more. My mouth gaped wide open as I watched the copse of trees that Anne and I had smooched in less than an hour ago growing rapidly larger in front of us.

Instinctively, I threw my arms up in front of my face as the huge ship ploughed into the small wood, sending entire trees soaring into the air as it gouged a huge tract in the hard, winter ground. The impact threw me forwards and I felt something break as I struck a console hard. My left arm exploded with pain and fell limp to my side. I screamed and the Greys screamed with me as the ship came to a juddering stop on the far side of the copse.

Struggling to my feet, I located the gun and picked it up, releasing the jammed clip, pulling out the spare and painfully ramming it home against my broken left forearm.

"Shut down the power plant. They must not retrieve this vessel in working order." The voice rang around my head like a peal of bells. I realized that the ship had not lost power during the attack as the walls were still very much transparent. My actions must have distracted the aliens from pulling the plug.

I saw one of the creatures reaching for a control and planted a bullet in its head without as much as a second thought. I backed away as the three surviving Greys advanced on me once more. I pointed my weapon at them, but they acted like cornered animals and had obviously decided to go out fighting.

I shot them in rapid succession, their skinny bodies flopping to the see-through deck like rag dolls. Throwing the gun away in disgust, I looked around the devastated wood and saw dozens of white and khaki figures running towards the ship. They ran past me and out of sight, so I decided to have a rest. I plopped into one of the tiny chairs and nursed my throbbing arm.

"Nice work, Lewis. You did a fine job."

"Piss off!" I told my controller and winced as more pain shot up my arm.

I glanced around at the dead bodies surrounding me and felt bile begin to rise in my throat once more. I felt as though I had murdered these beings in cold blood—and I probably had. Not one of them had been armed. I tried convincing myself that I had only been protecting myself, but I still felt incredible shame at my actions.

My shattered nerves slowly became aware of the sound of footsteps echoing from outside the control room. I did not look around as O'Donnell, Reese and a throng of technicians and soldiers appeared behind me, their forms unwrapping themselves from the illusory image at the back of the chamber. The captain rushed to my side and I grimaced when he accidentally brushed against my broken arm.

"Corporal Thompson, over here!" shouted O'Donnell and a young medic trotted across and began examining my aching limb.

"Does it hurt when I do this?" He squeezed my arm and I screamed in his face. "Okay, that's broken."

"I could've told you that, Corporal!" I said through clenched teeth. He reached into his pack and extracted a bleach-white sling. He tied it around the back of my neck and I painfully allowed him to slip my arm into its cradling cotton. "So, when do I get my Victoria Cross?"

"Sorry, Bill," smiled O'Donnell. "You're a civvie. You'll have to settle for the George Medal."

"Oh, goodie. Can I go home now?" I begged.

"Let's get that arm sorted first, eh?"

"Got a cigarette?" I asked feebly.

Miraculously, he did. I could have bore his children right there and then.

CHAPTER TWELVE

Anne threw herself into my arm and my eyes watered as she pressed against my injured limb. She kissed me firmly on the lips, relief and passion combining deliciously.

The well-equipped medical team had expertly set and bandaged my left arm and it was now resting painfully in a fresh sling. I was standing in the kitchen of the farmhouse with tears running down my cheeks, trying to explain to Anne that they were due to the pain of my injury. She knew me better than that.

"Was it as bad as it looked on the monitors?" she asked, sitting me down at the oak table.

Reese crossed to the stove and poured dark, pungent coffee into a large mug. He handed it to me and then retreated to a discreet distance in the hallway.

"It was terrible, Anne," I gushed and the tears really began to flow. I sniffed and she handed me a tissue. I blew my nose and peered at my ex-wife through red-rimmed eyes. "But, you know what the worst thing was?" She shook her head. "It wasn't that I thought that I was going to die. I'd pretty much accepted that by the time the ship started to go down. No, the worst part of it was that I thought that I'd never see you again."

"Oh, Bill." She took my right hand and stroked it as tears began to form in her own eyes.

"I love you," I admitted.

"Me too."

"What? You mean you love you as well?"

"No, you idiot. I love you, too, you dopey sod."

Suddenly, at this simple expression of affection, the realities of interstellar conflict paled into insignificance and I stared at Anne like a complete and utter moron—like you do when you are madly in love with someone.

"They're here," said Lieutenant Reese when a cacophony of sound burst through the open door.

We all rushed out into the farmyard, dust whirling in vibrant eddies around us. Six immense, double-rotored helicopters roared over our heads and came to hover above the UFO crash site. Thick, steel cables dangled from their bellies and each cable terminated in a huge hook.

"Do you really think they'll be able to lift that thing?" I asked, referring to the massive spacecraft lying in its shallow grave somewhere on the other side of the farmhouse.

"Oh, they'll lift it, Doctor Lewis," replied Reese confidently. He really loved his job, that one. "We've recovered bigger ones with the same equipment."

Suddenly another helicopter appeared on the scene. This one was not a military chopper, though, and its presence was definitely not welcome.

One of the Chinooks broke from formation and approached the rogue helicopter, its green and black form dwarfing the smaller aircraft. I could see a news cameraman hanging out of the door of the white and yellow chopper and desperately wished that he had got some good footage of the downed spaceship.

After a brief standoff, the civilian helicopter relented and swung around, leaving the scene as quickly as it had arrived.

"He'll never get that on the evening news," stated Reese smugly.

"You sound glad," I accused.

"Not at all, Doctor. I would be that first to cheer from the rooftops if all of this came out in the open. But the powers that be have decided that our knowledge is too sensitive for public consumption."

I sighed, a deep, weary exhalation. "Yeah, I suppose you're right."

Anne fired an angry look in my direction. "What do you mean by that?" she demanded.

I sensed one of our old arguments about to be reprised. Sod it, I thought and girded my loins. "Remember that meteorite they found with evidence of prehistoric Martian life inside?"

"Yes, I know where you're coming from," she replied. "And you're right."

I picked myself up off the floor and allowed her to continue.

She explained that when NASA had said that they had discovered the first evidence of extra-terrestrial life inside that meteorite, it had split the scientific community right down the middle. Half of them said, "Wow, that's fantastic!", while the other half had said that they did not believe it and that the data was flawed. It was generally thought that the same would apply to the general public if the world governments released conclusive proof that we were being visited and abducted by alien beings far more advanced than we. Half of the world would probably accept the information and get on with their daily routines, albeit a little more excited about life, while the other half would panic. There would be cultural shock on a global scale. Virtually all current religions would become obsolete and millions would be robbed of their faith—the Earth would no longer be the centre of God's universe. Many would most likely die, either by their own hand, incapable of living with this new truth, or by cult leaders and other nutters trying to hasten their own version of Judgement Day.

"So," Anne concluded, "the question is: Is it worth taking the risk and releasing the information all at once, or do you keep a very tight lid on it and only allow drips and drabs of the knowledge out when you feel that the public is ready for it?

"And I suppose the latter is the most sensible approach to take," she conceded.

I put my arm around her and gave her a gentle shake for encouragement. We continued to watch as the helicopters began to lift the alien craft from its resting place. The cables slowly became taut and, even from our position some distance from the operation, we could hear them cracking and popping with the strain placed upon them by the gargantuan load.

Then, in perfect unison, the six pilots gently increased power to their engines and the great vessel was delicately pulled from the ground. A dozen sets of enormous rotor blades hammered the air with mechanical fury as they struggled to haul their top-secret payload into the sky.

Then they were up and clear of the trees, an immense, black triangle swinging, passively beneath them. The

Chinooks continued to ascend until they were about two hundred feet above the ground. They then headed away from the crash site and into the darkening east.

I watched them go and wondered if the people would ever know of its existence. Would the cameraman ever get to show his film? Would the public believe it if he did? I made an insane decision and took Anne to one side, out of earshot of Reese.

"Fancy a drive into Waleford?" I asked innocently.

"Are you crazy?" she whispered back. "We wouldn't get five yards." She gestured towards the military roadblocks which had been set up on our arrival that morning. "Besides, how are we going to get there? On foot?"

"In that jeep over there. And Reese is coming with us."

I strolled towards our bodyguard and collapsed into the dust at his feet. Anne came rushing over as he kneeled to examine me.

"Has he passed out?" she asked virtuously.

"Looks like it," he replied. "Help me get him into the medical truck."

I tried to stay completely limp as they heaved and pulled me across the yard to a nearby wagon with a huge, red cross painted on its side. I hoped to God that they did not knock my broken arm or my ruse would be over as soon as it began. They bundled me inside and a doctor gave me a quick examination. I opened my eyes a fraction so that I could see what was going on.

"Is he all right?" Anne looked into the medic's eyes longingly.

"I'm not sure," admitted the doctor. "He seems okay, but he's totally unresponsive." He looked to Reese. "We could do to get him to a hospital. Get a jeep and tell the perimeter guards that Major Weiss has given you authorization to leave the area."

"Yessir." Lieutenant Reese dashed out of the trailer and returned two minutes later with the aforementioned jeep. The two officers lifted me from the medical truck and into the back of the tarpaulin-covered army vehicle.

"Can I go along?" asked Anne. I did not see it, but the major must have nodded because I heard two people climb into the car and its engine spluttered into life a second later.

I opened an eye fully and saw us pass through the roadblock, heading away from the farm. I had retrieved the pistol from the spacecraft's control room floor and had placed it back in the holster of my suit, instinctively folding the Velcro flap over its lethal form, before having my arm seen to. All of the electronic instruments had been removed from my person, as had the earplugs and contact lenses, during my first aid session. But, somehow, the weapon had been overlooked. I reached down and quietly pulled it free with my right hand. Slowly, I sat up and leaned forward, aiming the muzzle of the gun at the back of Reese's head.

"Hello, Lieutenant," I whispered. "I appear to have made a miraculous recovery." I noticed his hand go to his jacket. "Ah-aah, keep your hands on the wheel." I nudged the back of his neck with the cold gunmetal and he complied silently. "Now, I want you to drive us to the television station in Waleford."

"I don't know where it is."

"I do. I'll give you directions on the way."

"You're a dead man, Lewis," He said it matter-of-factly, as though it was an undisputed and inevitable part of my destiny. "O'Donnell is already on his way there. He probably has that film in his possession even as we speak. I assume that's why you want to go there—-to ensure that the film of the spacecraft is transmitted?"

"Just take us there," I insisted. I did not relish the thought of going up against Captain O'Donnell, but I was in too deep to back down now. "Anne, take his weapon."

She reached into Reese's jacket and pulled out his revolver. Cradling it in her lap uncertainly, she glanced back at me. "We're doing the right thing," she said, more to herself than anybody else.

I directed Reese to the television studio in the centre of Waleford. He drove efficiently and calmly, not drawing any unwanted attention to our vehicle in the rush hour traffic.

Eventually, we reached the station and passed through the security gate when Reese displayed his identification to the bemused guard. We parked in front of the main entrance, ignoring the signs that told us to do otherwise, and I climbed out of the back of the jeep, while Anne covered Reese with his own gun. I ordered the Orion man out of the automobile, my own pistol trained on him steadily. Anne tucked her weapon into the thick, woollen cardigan she was wearing. I nudged Reese to precede us and we walked awkwardly up the wide, stone steps that led to the shimmering, glass entrance hall.

Unknown to the lieutenant, I had slid my gun back into its concealing holster and had replaced it with my forefinger, which was jammed into the small of his back. I had no desire to be seen strolling around a major TV studio with a loaded gun in my hand. I only hoped that he didn't look round.

We approached the receptionist in the lobby and I shoved Reese forward with the muzzle of my .38 digit.

"Show her your ID and ask the way to the news cutting room," I whispered to him. He compliantly did as he was told.

"Are you here to meet Captain O'Donnell?" asked the receptionist cheerfully.

I started at the mention of the name and gave Reese another nudge when he failed to answer for a second.

"Yes, that's correct," he said flatly.

She pointed us in the right direction and we set off down a long, wide corridor. I seemed to be spending my entire life in long corridors these days. Climbing a flight of stairs at the end, we saw O'Donnell about to enter a room a few yards down the passage.

"Captain," I called. "Don't go in there."

He turned to face us, an expression of surprise on his chiselled visage. "Lewis! Reese! What the hell are you doing here?"

We slowly approached the confused officer and I hastily pulled out the pistol and quickly replaced my finger with it.

"He's got a gun, sir," said Reese. "He's gone crazy."

"All right, Lewis. Stop right there." O'Donnell drew his own weapon and pointed its black barrel in my direction. "Drop the gun, or you die where you stand."

Luckily for me, Reese's muscled bulk was between myself and the wicked-looking muzzle of the captain's revolver. "I don't think so, Captain," I replied. My knees had turned to jelly and I was sweating profusely in the jumpsuit. "You drop yours."

"You know that's not going to happen, Lewis."

Suddenly a kaleidoscope of colours burst across my field of vision and pain exploded throughout my left arm. Reese had jabbed his elbow into my injured limb and grabbed my weapon as I screamed in agony. I sank to my knees, nursing my throbbing arm, tears rolling down my face.

I felt something cold against my forehead and looked up. Reese had my own gun pressed into the crease between my eyebrows and was glaring down at me with undisguised hate in his eyes.

I heard a gunshot and fell back onto the tiled floor, fully expecting to meet my grandparents at any minute. Instead, I opened my eyes and saw Reese lying in a rapidly expanding pool of his own blood.

"Drop it, lady!" I heard O'Donnell roar and looked around to see Anne standing a few feet behind me, Reese's revolver smoking in her trembling hands.

"No! You put your gun on the floor and kick it to Bill," she ordered, her voice wavering with sheer terror. When O'Donnell failed to comply, she pulled back the hammer of her pistol. "I'll shoot!" she proclaimed.

The captain slowly bent forward and gently placed his gun by his feet. Then he kicked it with a shiny boot and it slid across the floor, coming to rest by my knees. I picked it up and staggered to my feet as a head appeared at the cutting room door.

"Oh my God!" exclaimed the bespectacled man upon seeing Reese's inert, but still breathing, form.

"Call the police," I yelled. "And an ambulance." His head vanished and the door slammed, echoing as loudly as had the gunshot.

Footsteps on the stairs behind us caused me to turn and see dozens of people following a security guard into the corridor. They stopped together, stunned by the scene before them.

The man reappeared at the door next to O'Donnell, who had placed his hands on his head at Anne's insistence. "They're on their way," he reported.

Then I remembered what I was here for. "The film from the Biggins' farm?" I enquired.

"I'll get it," said the terrified editor.

"No!" I shouted. "You've got to broadcast it as soon as possible."

"It was due to be the main headline for the six o'clock news," replied the man.

I looked at my watch. It was five to six. "Go! Do your job." He vanished and I stared at O'Donnell. "It'll be over soon. The whole world will know about the Greys."

"You're making a big mistake, Lewis," he snarled.

I shrugged and listened as sirens grew steadily louder outside. I checked my watch again. Six o'clock.

Two paramedics pushed their way through the crowd and rushed to Reese. They examined him with expert haste and began applying pressure to the bullet wound in his shoulder.

"He's lost a lot of blood," said one of the paramedics to his colleague. "He'll die if we don't get him to the hospital fast."

At that precise moment, Reese let out a strangled cry and his chest ceased rising. The paramedics tried frantically to revive him, but eventually stood up, dejected.

"He's dead," the first medic stated. Anne breathed in sharply and I knew what she was going through. At least she hadn't thrown up, yet.

"All right, everybody. Move back."

The police had arrived and were hustling the crowd back down the stairs. When the mob was safely cleared, two uniformed constables took up positions at the top of the steps, warily eyeing mine and Anne's weapons, still trained on O'Donnell.

Then a man dressed in civilian clothes arrived and pushed his way by the uniforms. I recognized him as Detective Sergeant McCloud, the man who was investigating the Biggins suicide'.

"Okay, everybody stay calm." He spoke in hushed, appeasing tones. "Now, sir, miss, give me the guns."

I handed him my weapon promptly and told Anne to do likewise. McCloud looked stunned by our subservient cooperation. He glanced across at our former prisoner.

"Captain O'Donnell, would you care to explain what is going on here?"

"No," he replied succinctly. "Arrest these two and charge them with the murder of Lieutenant Reese." Then he rushed into the cutting room and returned a minute later, holding a videocassette. However, his face looked exceedingly glum. He regarded me with contempt as McCloud snapped the handcuffs around my right wrist and locked the other half around Anne's left. "Well, you got your wish. The footage was broadcast. Now, we'll have to see if we can tidy up the mess you've left behind." He peered down at the body of his partner and his bottom lip quivered slightly. "Now I've got to tell Martin's wife the bad news." I had a vision of a dusty stamp collection as O'Donnell shoved past me and trudged down the steps.

The paramedics gently lifted Reese's body onto a stretcher and covered him with a spotless, white sheet. We waited until they had gone and then the policemen bundled us downstairs and into a waiting van.

"You okay?" I asked as we sat on the hard, wooden bench in the back of the armoured vehicle.

"Not really," Anne replied, her head bowed. "I've just murdered someone."

"No you didn't," I countered. "He had his gun to my head, remember?"

"I still feel like shit." She looked into my watery eyes. "Bill, why did you want to do this? I thought you were dead against the public receiving knowledge of the aliens?"

"I thought, *what the hell...* Do we really have the right to keep something like this a secret?"

The van began moving and Anne looked to the police officer sat opposite.

"What will happen to us now?" She turned her gaze upon me when he did not answer.

"Don't know," I replied honestly. "Maybe the Greys will rescue us."

CHAPTER THIRTEEN

Salvation comes from the most unlikely sources. No sooner had we been interrogated, charged and thrown into the cells of Waleford Metropolitan Police Station, than we were out again, whisked away in a plain, black Granada, first thing the next morning.

I leaned forward and asked the driver where we were being taken. He ignored me. In fact, he went so far as to press a button to raise a thick piece of soundproof glass, sealing Anne and I in our new, leather-trimmed cell.

Anne looked at me with wide, concerned eyes. "What do you think?"

"Me?" I replied. "I think Quentin-Smythe is behind this. The transmission of the crashed UFO film has put a rather hefty spanner in his works and he probably wants me to answer for it."

"Then, why didn't he just leave you at the mercy of the justice system? We had been charged with Reese's murder."

"If we had gone to court, then we would have spilled the beans about Smythe and his Orion group." I took a deep breath. "They couldn't take the risk." I pulled out a pack of cigarettes. Detective Sergeant McCloud had supplied them during my initial interrogation. I had told him all about the Orion Committee, but I doubted his belief—and I bet that Smythe's cronies had grabbed the tapes of the interview as well. I lit one of the cigarettes and puffed calmly. "Besides, what's been shown anyway?"

"What do you mean?"

"All that was transmitted was an image of a large, black, triangular object nestled in a huge gouge in the middle of a small wood." I inhaled more smoke.

"But they can't deny it now," Anne ventured hopefully.

"Just watch them," I said and tried, unsuccessfully, to wind down the side window. "I'll bet you a thousand pounds that they say it was some top secret stealth bomber that crashed." Another puff. "Just wait and see." I raised a wise eyebrow.

We stared blankly out of the tinted panes of glass as the city swept by, soon to be replaced by hedgerows and patchwork fields, rushing past at fifty miles per hour. It was the road to the Biggins' farm.

We both looked as the farmyard sped by. It was completely empty. All of the trailers had been removed and even the deep ruts that they had left in the mud had been smoothed over and replaced with authentic-looking tractor tyre grooves. There was no trace at all of the Orion Committee's presence the day before.

I peered into the fields behind the farmhouse and saw that the entire copse, where the UFO had crashed, had been razed to the ground. All that remained was an ugly tract of ploughed earth.

"By God, they're efficient," I remarked, impressed and at the same time depressed by Smythe's expeditious professionalism.

We raced on and, just over an hour later, we pulled off the road and drove through a set of huge, iron gates. A long, gravel drive extended for several hundred yards in front of us and at the end stood an imposing Edwardian mansion. Acres of wooded grounds surrounded the house, giving it an air of quiet seclusion.

Our mute driver pulled up outside the broad front of the edifice, at the base of a mighty flight of steps, and climbed out. He opened the door on my side and Anne and I shuffled out, squinting in the bright, morning sunshine. He then climbed back into the car and drove away towards the rear of the house, leaving us standing like tourists on the bottom step.

"Oh well," I said optimistically. "We might as well see if anyone's in."

I took Anne's hand and we started up the stairs towards a heavy, wooden door. I was about to use the massive, brass knocker, when the door opened and a butler leered at us from behind wire-frame spectacles.

"Morning, Jeeves," I smiled. He harrumphed and stepped back to afford us entry.

We found ourselves in a cavernous lobby. Two ornate staircases swept upwards to the first floor and as our impressed eyes followed its path, we beheld a mighty chandelier, hanging like a supernova above our heads.

Jeeves led us to an adjoining room and proclaimed that Sir Donald Quentin-Smythe would join us shortly. Then he left, closing the double doors behind him.

I gave Anne an 'I told you so' look and proceeded to explore the room. It was an elegantly furnished library;

thousands of expensive-looking books lined the walls and a precarious ladder enabled access to the uppermost shelves. I felt like Cary Grant in North by Northwest. In fact, I half expected James Mason and Martin Landau to stroll in and start opening a bottle of whiskey for me. I told Anne of my delusions and she giggled nervously. I continued my survey of the area.

A large, mahogany desk dominated the room and three simple, utilitarian chairs were arranged around it. One was behind the desk, its back to a monstrous picture window, and the other two were on our side. I strolled around the desk, which was empty save for an old-fashioned looking, black telephone, and absorbed the view through the leaded glass.

A wide expanse of lawn stretched into the near distance with a line of tall pines bordering its perimeter. A robin fluttered onto the patio outside and regarded me with black, suspicious eyes. I smiled at it and the creature flew away, totally unimpressed. I had always had that effect on the birds.

I heard the double doors open behind me and turned to see Smythe enter the room. The expression on his face looked like it had been drawn onto paper, cut out and glued onto the front of his head. He was not a happy bunny.

“Sit down,” he ordered tersely as he came around the desk.

“What? No cucumber sandwiches?” I mocked, returning to Anne’s side and perching on the nearest seat.

Anne sat on the other chair, her eyes flitting around the library in an agitated frenzy.

Smythe breathed deeply and sat down, the dark wood a comfortable barrier between us. He regarded us with angry, piercing pupils.

"You've created a fine old mess, Doctor Lewis," he said finally.

"Just following my instincts," I smiled back.

Smythe leapt to his feet, his face shaking like an unappetizing jelly. "You killed one of my men!" he exploded.

"He had a gun pressed to my forehead!" I exploded back, also rising to my feet. "Did you expect us to sit back and be perforated by your trigger happy goons?"

"Reese wouldn't have shot you. He was too well trained."

"Well, I'm sorry, but I can't read minds," I retorted. Anne was shuffling uncomfortably on her chair. I sat back down and took her hand. "So, what's going to happen to us now?" I had lowered my voice by a hundred decibels or so.

Sir Donald returned to his seat, relieved that I was not going to dive over the desk and strangle him. He steepled his fingers in front of him and blew out a steady stream of air.

"Well?" I insisted.

"I'm not entirely sure, Doctor. I suppose that I could have you both shot through the head and dumped somewhere." I admired his honesty, but tensed at his words nevertheless. "But I think that there's been enough killing lately. Don't you?"

I nodded, a little unnerved by his sudden passiveness. He folded his arms and leaned back in the chair, its legs creaking ominously.

"I've been on the phone to the PM all morning," he said eventually. "He wanted to know what all this was about a crashed alien spaceship."

"The Prime Minister doesn't know?" I asked, amazed.

"Of course he doesn't," muttered Anne. She gazed into Smythe's eyes. "Sir Donald here's a civil servant. Ministers come and go, but the Civil Service plods on year after year, administration after administration. They're the ones with the real power."

"You should work for us permanently," said Smythe appreciatively. "With your insight, you could go far in The Service."

"Hah!" she snorted back and fell silent once more. I could tell that speaking to this odious scumbag had a detrimental effect on her mood.

"Anyway," continued Sir Donald. "Thanks to help from our American friends, we have informed him that a US Air Force B-2 Stealth Bomber executed an emergency landing outside Waleford, killing the crew and levelling a local beauty spot." He smiled without conviction. "He will appear on national television tonight and issue a statement to that effect."

"You've really got it all covered," I said. "It will all be brushed under the carpet and the public will forget about it in no time."

"Our group hasn't been in operation for over fifty years without learning how to lie convincingly." He leaned forward. "But, the point is, that thanks to your reckless actions, there could have been a major security scare and widespread public panic."

"Come on!" I said. "For nearly twelve hours now, the public has believed that a flying saucer has crashed into a farmer's field and that the government has retrieved it. I don't hear any panic out there. Give the people some credit."

"Doctor Lewis, the public deserve no credit whatsoever." He smiled ingratiatingly. God, I hated this man. I shifted uncomfortably on my seat. "The general populace of any country are like sheep. As individual entities, people can absorb and cope with almost anything. But when they are part of a large group, mass hysteria sets in and they get swept along on a tide of anarchy."

"You don't really believe that?" spat Anne. "How can you have such outright contempt for people?"

"Mrs. Lewis, I have the utmost respect for the individuals who pay my salary." He steepled his fingers again as he sat back in his chair. "But the theory is sound. It is a matter of tidal forces, wouldn't you agree, Doctor Lewis?"

I nodded, completely grasping the theory of which he was speaking. Everybody knows that the moon (and to a lesser degree, the sun) affects the tides. In fact, if there were no moon, there would be no tides. But what is not generally known is that the gravitational pull of the moon on the Earth is infinitesimal. A sheet of paper has more gravitational attraction on us than our own satellite. That is why minor bodies of water such as lakes and small seas have no tides—only vast oceans and seas with gargantuan volumes of water are affected by the moon's tugging embrace. It is like a domino effect: the moon pulls on one molecule of water, which in turn pulls on its neighbour and so on. When you have a large body of liquid several miles deep and thousands of miles across, then the result is obvious. But with lakes only a few feet deep, there is not enough water to create a tide.

Smythe was saying that people were like this. Individually, one person has little impact on his surroundings. But, in large groups, if some of them panic, the emotion will spread to their companions and, very quickly, a dangerous and highly volatile situation could occur.

Anne glared at me as I explained this to her, obviously not concurring with my summation. To her credit, though, she eventually shrugged and redirected her poisonous gaze back to Quentin-Smythe. I breathed a sigh of relief. A considerable amount of respect for her had grown in me over the past days and I liked my lovebuds just the way they were. I decided to change the subject slightly.

"So, where have you taken the ship? The airbase?"

"That is correct. A team of scientists is going over it with a fine toothcomb. Doctor Tovey is in charge of the investigation." Smythe's eyes began to twinkle and I knew that something bad was on its way. "There is some better news, though."

I raised an eyebrow at him. "I think I know what's coming, but go on," I quavered. My rectum was twitching like a rabbit's nose.

"Five members of the crew survived the crash. They were in what we believe is the engine room. They were all knocked unconscious when the ship impacted and our team extracted them before they awoke."

"Is the vessel still functioning?" asked Anne.

"Oh yes," he replied. "And the footage you provided of the Greys in the control room has given our men valuable insight into the ship's operating systems."

"And the aliens?" she said. "They are well? You are treating them fairly?"

"Of course. They have received the best medical attention and are being detained in secure but comfortable accommodations." He leaned forward again, his elbows on the desk. "Unfortunately, none of our linguistics team has been able to communicate with them. Either they are not willing to speak to us, or they are unable to. Doctor Lewis..."

"You want me to talk to them." I lit a cigarette and puffed furiously.

"Yes." He reached into a drawer and handed me a marble ashtray. "The Greys have spoken to you before telepathically. Perhaps they will do so again."

"I thought that you had captured dozens of these aliens before?" I flicked a lump of carbonised tobacco into the ashtray. "Don't tell me that after fifty years, your boffins still haven't found a way to communicate with them."

"On the contrary, there have been numerous meetings where successful discourse has occurred. The problem is that the Greys are a very peculiar bunch." He tapped the side of his head with a bony index finger. "It seems that they only talk to us when they will get something out of it for themselves. Perhaps, as you are not an official member of our group, they will speak to you more openly."

"I killed six of their crew and punched another one in the face. I don't think that I'll be top of their visitor's list."

"They'll have no idea who you are. All of the aliens in our care were found in the engine room. You were nowhere near that section when you were aboard their ship."

"Believe me, Smythe, they'll know exactly who I am."

"Will you do it?" he asked, smiling.

"You keep asking me if I'll do all of these crazy things! We all know that I have no choice." I took another drag from the cigarette. "Of course I'll do it, or at least try."

Smythe clapped his hands. "Jolly good. We will leave for the facility first thing tomorrow morning. In the meantime, you are welcome to enjoy the house and grounds. Jennings will show you to your rooms."

Right on cue, the doors opened and the miserable, old butler entered. We left the smug, smiling, fistable face of Smythe in his library and were shown up the wide staircase to the first floor. Jennings led us down a long, dim corridor—all wood panelling and portraits of morose-looking men and women dressed in period costume. He stopped by a dark, wooden door and we almost piled into the back of him.

"This is madam's room," he said dismally as he opened the door. "Your room is this way, sir."

He shuffled to the next door and I scraped along just behind. He opened it and showed me inside. "Madam's is the next room, through the connecting door." He pointed to a portal in the wall opposite my bed and turned to leave, the air of dejection around him almost palpable.

"Tell me, Jennings. Do you get a lot of satisfaction from your job?"

"No, sir, I do not. Dinner is at seven." He left slowly and I felt like hanging myself.

I studied my surroundings and felt little better. The room was dominated by a huge four-poster bed, complete with drapes and, probably, the ghost of Anne Boleyn. I just hoped she didn't snore.

I walked to the window, snorted and grunted whilst trying to open it, but finally settled on looking through the dusty glass. Acres of lawn stretched below me and in the distance I could see a man riding one of those motorised mowers. I tried the window again and this time, after more sweating and spitting, it opened noisily. Fresh, country air poured into my nostrils and the drone of the mower could be heard as it made its way across the prairie. I flicked out my cigarette and closed the window again, gritting my teeth as it screeched back down.

Turning around, I walked over to the bed and sat down, the ancient springs creaking angrily at me. On the small bedside cabinet was an old lamp, its shade yellow and dusty with age, and a bible. I picked up the book and leafed through it absently. Smythe did not strike me as the religious type, but I gave him the benefit of the doubt.

I looked up as the connecting door opened and Anne stepped into my room. She crossed to my side of the bed, taking my hand and looking around the chamber.

"Kind of depressing this place," she stated. "I feel like Jane Eyre or someone out of a Dickens novel."

"I feel like a shower or a bath. Did Jennings, the laughing butler, happen to tell you where we could clean up?" She shook her head. "Then let's go exploring."

CHAPTER FOURTEEN

We went out into the corridor and tried all the doors that we could find. Two of them were unlocked. One was a cleaning cupboard and the other was a tiny bathroom with a large, brown-stained tub and no towels. We decided to find some assistance.

We swept down the staircase, the chandelier swaying gently above us, and went into the library. It was empty, Smythe had gone. Returning to the hall, I saw several other doors on the far side and dragged Anne towards them. I turned the handle of the first door that we came to. It opened creakily.

Inside was a large ballroom affair, but instead of a dance floor, the room was almost completely filled by an enormous conference table. There were some typed pages neatly placed at regular intervals around the table, in front of the thirty or so chairs. The room was as devoid of life as the library. I grabbed one of the wads of paper and crammed it into my one-piece suit, winking at Anne.

"Some bedtime reading," I quipped.

"Can I help you, sir?"

We both started at the voice. Turning around, we saw Jennings hunched in the doorway.

"Er, yes." I cleared my throat. "We were looking for you. I was wondering where we might get some soap and towels and a change of clothes."

He looked me up and down, as though I was a new slave, just bought by the master and ready to set to work.

"Follow me."

He took us back to our rooms and opened the drawers in our bedside cabinets. Fresh, clean towels resided there and a polythene-wrapped cake of soap sat patiently on top of them. Jennings then pulled open the wardrobe doors to display a variety of clothing. Men's in my room and women's in Anne's.

"If sir had taken the time to search his immediate surroundings, then sir would have found the towels." He left the room, muttering under his stale breath, and closed the door behind him.

"If sir had taken the time..." I mimicked. "Miserable old bugger!" If there is one thing that I cannot stand, it's crabby old people.

I strode into Anne's room, using the connecting door, and saw a towel disappearing into the corridor.

"Why don't you go first," I called.

"Thanks," echoed the reply.

I returned to my room and sat back on the bed. I pulled the papers from my tunic and stashed them beneath one of the fluffy pillows. Then I retrieved a towel and the soap and waited for Anne to finish in the bathroom. Knowing my ex-wife, I would be in for a long wait, so I lay down and closed my eyes.

I opened them again when I felt pressure on my lips and dampness on my face. I saw Anne kissing me, her wet hair leaving damp streaks across my cheeks. Just as I was starting to enjoy myself, she pulled back and smiled down at me.

"I've finished," she said.

"Typical. Just as it was getting good."

"I mean in the bathroom, silly."

"Did I doze off?" She nodded and I checked my watch. "You've been in there for two hours!"

"I was dirty."

"So was Nixon, but I bet he didn't spend two hours in the bath." I sat up and grabbed my toiletries. "I'll get cleaned up and then we can go for a walk before dinner, eh?"

I kissed her and skipped from the chamber, coming back a second later and choosing some clothes from the wardrobe.

"How come Smythe has all these clothes that just happen to fit us?" I asked.

"It's all a conspiracy," said Anne, grinning beautifully.

I grinned back and went to bathe.

Fifteen minutes later, I returned wearing jeans, shirt, a pair of squeaky, new sneakers and feeling totally refreshed. Somehow, a night in the cells leaves you feeling incredibly grubby. I decided at that moment that I would concentrate more on penal reform. Maybe not.

Anne had changed into a cotton skirt and blouse and was wearing a pair of comfortable sandals. She had dried her hair, applied a little make-up (she had never needed much—she had that kind of face) and looked absolutely ravishing. This was all the more incredible considering that she had spent the previous night in the cell next to me charged with murder. I took her hand and we swept down the staircase like Rhett and Scarlett and sashayed out of the front doors.

The grounds stretched before us to the horizon, the vast lawn broken by uninhabited flowerbeds. To the left and right, a gravel path led round to the back of the mansion and we decided to follow the right hand one. At the side of the house, the lawns were replaced by thick shrubbery—rhododendrons and such—and at the rear, the pine forest almost met the drive, upon which were parked several large, black cars and the limousine in which we were brought here. A narrow path disappeared into the trees and we took it, the house soon vanishing from sight behind us.

We walked for over half an hour, talking about trivial things: it's a nice day; the trees are tall; are we going to die? That sort of thing. The forest seemed to go on forever—Smythe's estate was huge. I supposed being the head of a super-secret government organization had its perks.

Eventually, we came to a high, wire-mesh fence. This was obviously the boundary to our keeper's domain. The path split into three at this point. One way went left, one right and the third disappeared back the way we had come. The sun was descending rapidly, so we decided to retrace our steps and return to the main house. As we walked, the forest grew darker, more menacing and when the mansion loomed into view, we both breathed a heavy sigh of relief. We double-timed it round to the front of the house and stepped into the hall only to be met by Quentin-Smythe himself.

"Ah, there you are," he greeted. "I was about to send Jennings looking for you. Enjoy your stroll?"

"Very pleasant," I admitted. "The grounds are quite magnificent."

“Yes,” started Anne. “This place must cost the taxpayers a pretty penny.” I nudged her with my elbow. I was in no mood for another one of her morality speeches. “But money well spent,” she concluded upon seeing my stern gaze.

Smythe smiled his insincere smile. By God, what I would not have given for some rough sandpaper and a bottle of rubbing alcohol. I would get immense pleasure from scouring his face off.

My sadistic train of thought was broken by the sound of tyres crunching on gravel. We followed Smythe outside and saw Tovey climbing out of one of the omni-present black cars. How many of those things did the Orion Committee have? And who the hell manufactured them? I doubted they rented their fleet from Hertz.

After depositing its passenger at the foot of the steps, the car scrunched away to the back of the house and Tovey vaulted up to the front door, his black tie flapping wildly around his face. He shook our keeper’s hand warmly and eyed Anne and I suspiciously. I supposed that he had expected us to be locked in police cells, not hobnobbing with his employer.

“Graeme, you’re just in time for dinner,” enthused Smythe. As he was led into the house, Tovey continued his distrustful staring over his shoulder. I suppressed the urge to stick my tongue out at him, then thought, *what the hell*, and stuck my tongue out at him.

As we stepped back into the hall, Jennings appeared near a door at the back of the cavernous chamber and declared, in a weary voice, that dinner was served. I must admit that I was starving. Our host may have given us first-class accommodation, but he had sorely overlooked our nutritional needs. Our last meal had been a greasy fry-up, courtesy of Her Majesty's Constabulary, first thing that morning. Jennings neatly sidestepped out of the way as we rushed after Smythe and Tovey into the dining room.

"Jennings, set an extra place for Dr. Tovey," ordered Smythe.

The butler grumbled an affirmation and shuffled off to the kitchen. Anne smiled at me, amused by the servant's constantly down-at-heal manner. I, on the other hand was staring, watery-eyed, through the dining room doors.

A veritable banquet was laid out on the huge, oak table and I was assailed by the image of Henry VIII tucking into cooked chicken legs whilst plotting to decapitate his latest wife.

"This way, sir." I jumped with shock as Jennings barged past me, carrying fresh plates and cutlery, and gestured for Anne and me to follow.

We were led to the far end of the table, where Smythe had taken his seat at its head, the squire of his particular manor. Tovey was sitting to his right and we were shown to our places on the civil servant's left. I had barely unfolded my neatly pressed napkin when a bowl of steaming soup appeared before me, closely followed by a small plate containing a solitary bread roll.

I attacked the roll, tearing it to shreds, and plunged its tattered remains into my pea soup. Smythe, Tovey and Anne stared at me incredulously for a moment and then set about their own first courses at a more sedate pace. I mopped up the last of my soup, then sat back and belched loudly. Anne kicked me under the table and I yelped with pain, but did not protest when I saw her reproachful stare.

When everybody had finished, the butler removed the empty dishes and informed us that the main course would be along presently. Smythe obviously took this as the cue to indulge in small talk.

"So then, Graeme, how are things going?"

Tovey studied his placemat furiously, his avoidance of Smythe's eyes speaking volumes. "Er, slight hitch on that front," he stammered. Anne and I craned forward. "One of the technicians inadvertently shut down the power to the alien craft and we, er, can't get it going again."

I was loving this.

"What?" Smythe exploded out of his seat, upsetting his wine glass. "I do not believe that I heard you correctly, Dr. Tovey."

Tovey fidgeted with his fork. "We were trying to decipher the alien symbols in the engine room using standard sequential methodology..."

"You mean trial and error'," I interjected.

"... and it appears that we somehow isolated the power plant from the rest of the ship's systems."

"In short, Graeme, you pushed the wrong button." Smythe buried his face into his hands. "Why didn't you call Majestic and have them send a team of philologists over? That is standard procedure. Well it was the last time I read the manuals."

"I did make the call, sir. They will arrive in two days time, but..."

"But you just couldn't wait, could you?" Smythe exploded again. He calmed back down almost immediately, this time. "So, the ship has no power whatsoever?"

Tovey's eyes seemed to twinkle as he saw a ray of hope. "Sir Donald, I believe that you've misunderstood me. The power plant is still on-line, as is a single control station in the engine room. All we need to do is find the correct sequence to reactivate the rest of the ship."

"Well, I suggest you get back there and work on it." Smythe lowered himself back down and composed himself. He closed his eyes and then opened them a second later. "Are you still here, Doctor?"

Tovey bolted out of his chair and barrelled out of the room, almost knocking Jennings over as he brought our next course into the dining room. The inscrutable butler placed several tureens onto the table and left, mumbling about clumsy flaming scientists.

"Bloody idiot." Smythe ran his slender fingers through his grey hair and looked at me. I was hiding a smirk with my hand, but our host was in no mood for jollity. "I'm glad you find this amusing, Dr. Lewis."

"Oh, come on, Sir Donald. It's hilarious." I began scooping vegetables onto my plate and then turned my attention to the slab of beef residing quietly in the centre of the table. "Something like this was bound to happen when you put a man like Graeme Tovey in charge." I plonked several large slices of cow on top of my carrots and soaked them with thick, brown gravy. "But you can't blame him really."

"Why not?"

"He's dealing with a technology that is totally alien to us, if you'll forgive the pun. There are bound to be some set-backs." I stuffed in a mouthful of meat and munched greedily.

Smythe helped himself to the food, as did Anne, and we sat in masticating silence for several minutes. The meal was delicious and when I had finished (before everybody else, I might add) I belched again and lit a cigarette, ignoring Anne's gaze.

“There may be a way to get the ship up and running again if the Majestic guys can’t do it.” I blew a steady stream of smoke over Smythe’s head.

“Really, how?” He set down his cutlery and regarded me intently.

“I’m sure the Greys could tell us the correct command sequence to restart the ship.”

Quentin-Smythe laughed out loud and handed me an ashtray when he saw me flick ash onto my plate. “What makes you think that they will help us? We have been unable to get anything out of them. They totally refuse to communicate with us.”

“Maybe I can talk to them,” I ventured. “You said that you wanted me to try to speak with them anyway. They are proud, but not stupid. I’m sure that I can reason with them. If not...”

“Yes?”

“If not, you could always threaten to shoot one of them.”

“Bill!” Anne was on her feet. “How could you even suggest such a thing?”

I raised my hands and gently sat her back down. “I said we could threaten to shoot one of them, not actually do it.”

“What makes you think that they will tell us what we need to know? They may be prepared to die before divulging their secrets to a lesser race.”

“Perhaps that is so, Sir Donald.” I stubbed out the cigarette, a thin stream of smoke rose perfectly vertical from the ashtray. “But I get the impression that they value their own lives above all else. We may be lab rats to them, but they do have some lingering respect for us.” I sighed. “And they know what we are capable of.”

“But the Greys on the ship attacked you,” said Anne.

"I had them backed into a corner," I replied. "They had no choice but to have a go at me. Their situation now is very different."

"Very well, Dr. Lewis, we will try your plan. Ah, here comes the dessert."

After our coffee ice cream, we were ordered back to our rooms and told to get a good night's sleep. We were going to have an early start the next day.

I saw Anne to her room and kissed her gently on the cheek before ensuring that she locked her door behind her. Entering my own bedchamber, I secured the door and slumped down onto the edge of the bed. Then I remembered the documents that I had secreted under my pillow. I fished them out and shuffled through the official-looking pages. I was shocked by what I read.

According to the briefing documents, a state of hostilities had existed between the Earth and the Greys since the early seventies. Soon after the conclusion of World War Two, our governments had secretly begun research into the vast number of UFO sightings and had actually succeeded in contacting the Greys face to face. An understanding had been reached and we allowed them to use our airspace unmolested in return for certain concessions—one of them being the exchange of limited technologies.

Unfortunately, the aliens had not been entirely forthcoming with us. In the early sixties, the contact between our peoples inexplicably ceased and the human abductions began. A decade of fruitless attempts at re-establishing contact ended with the discovery of a concealed Grey base deep beneath the Nevada desert.

Special military forces, attached to Majestic Twelve, stormed the subterranean facility and made a gruesome discovery. Huge chambers were filled from floor to ceiling with row upon row of clear, liquid-filled cylinders. Within each of these receptacles floated the perfectly preserved and quite lifeless forms of hundreds of humans. Men, women and even children had been taken by the Greys and experimented upon. The documents didn't go into details about the nature of these experiments, but I could imagine something quite horrific.

The Greys had attempted to defend themselves and their base using strange, radiation based weapons, but they had stood no chance against the unleashed fury of man. Over three hundred aliens had been executed that day and sixteen soldiers died later from wounds inflicted by the extra-terrestrials' weapons.

That had been in 1974 and since then, Majestic Twelve and the Orion Committee had been charged with ridding the Earth of its alien menace. Unfortunately, they had not been doing very well. The abductions continued and UFO reports were on the increase. Now the Greys were butchering our livestock and removing certain organs for their own consumption. If they were taking foodstuffs from Earth, the papers stated, then that meant only one thing—they were here to stay. At least for the time being.

The more I read, the more certain I was that we were not dealing with some benevolent, sage race, as Anne believed. Rather, I got the impression that out planet and its dominant species, humans, were being studied as a prelude to some sort of invasion.

Then I recalled the impressions that had been planted in my mind during my own abduction. I had received the image that it was humans who were the invaders, that the Earth was originally possessed by the Greys and that somehow, in the distant past, we had either wrested control from them or they had left of their own accord, not expecting the land to be occupied when they returned.

But there was more to this than met the eye. During my abduction, I had been given the notion that they did not exactly like the things that we had done with the Earth. We had spoiled it for them. Perhaps it needed cleansing before they returned en masse, I thought. Could that mean that they intended to exterminate the human race?

An ice-cold shiver ran the length of my spine. For the first time, I was glad that Majestic and Orion existed to fight for our survival and I silently promised to assist them as much as I could, despite their often savage methods.

I decided not to show the documents to Anne. She would think that they were propaganda and misinformation. She was of the opinion that it was the Greys who were the victims and that we were the barbarians waging war on them for our own power hungry ends.

I slid the papers back under my pillow and, after undressing, climbed beneath the cool, cotton sheets. I left the lamp on and soon fell into a disturbed slumber, visions of large, grey, oval heads and huge, black, almond eyes swimming behind my eyelids.

CHAPTER FIFTEEN

We were roused the following morning by the Butler from the Black Lagoon. I thought he was attempting to break down the door, so forceful was his rapping. A light breakfast of tea and toast with Sir Donald preceded our journey to the airbase.

To my surprise, we were not transported in one of the eponymous black cars. A gleaming, white Rolls Royce was waiting at the foot of the steps, as were two military police motorcycles. The grim-faced chauffeur held the nearside rear door open and the three of us climbed in. The door closed and seconds later we were on our way, the motorcycles providing escort to the front and rear.

The interior of the Roller was more luxurious than my house (which wasn't too surprising now I think about it). A drinks cabinet chinked enticingly in front of us and to either side was a television screen and a top of the range hi-fi system. Smythe did not offer us a tipple, nor did he switch on one of the entertainment facilities. He merely sat and smiled at me.

"Is there a problem, Sir Donald?" I asked innocently. I suspected that I was in trouble about something, but could not figure out what.

"Did you enjoy your night reading?" he replied smugly.

"Sorry?"

"The briefing document you stole. Did you find it illuminating?"

"Oh, that," I conceded. I should have realized that the documents would have been missed. "Yes, they were very interesting." I cast a sideways glance to Anne.

"Well?" she said, sensing my reticence.

"Well what?"

"What did they say?" I could tell that she was growing angry, knowing that I was withholding something from her.

"I'd rather not say," I mumbled. "There were some pretty scary things in those papers."

"You're beginning to sound like him." She shot an icicle glare at Smythe and his smile shattered like a super-cooled sphincter. "You've been associated with these goons for a few weeks and already you're playing along with their secrecy games. You're as bad as they..."

"That's enough!" I snapped. "Don't you ever tarnish me with the same brush as them"

She folded her arms across her chest, obviously disdained by my use of such a common metaphor. I was angry and couldn't think of anything more creative at the time.

Smythe pouted at me and shook his head. I knew then that my decision had been made. Reaching into my inside jacket pocket, I withdrew the folded documents that I had stuffed there that morning and handed them to Anne. She turned them over in her hands and looked at me.

"Go on, read them," I ordered. Smythe looked to the skies and shook his head again. "But don't blame me if what you find in there disturbs you."

She scanned through the papers quietly, licking her fingers as she turned each page. As she read, I took the opportunity to look out of the window. I saw by the road signs that we were heading north into Yorkshire. I'd guessed that the secret base was somewhere in the north of England, judging by the accents of the locals we had encountered in Cranbourne. Until now, I'd had no way of confirming my theory—road atlases had been the last things on my mind recently.

As Anne read, the motorway dissolved and we continued our five-star journey on narrower country lanes, hedgerows and green fields whipping by at an unnerving velocity. Small towns and villages soon gave way to open heathland and I knew that we were coming to the end of our trek. My stomach muscles tightened and a wave of nausea swept over me. The thought of entering that sterile facility again filled me with dread. But, more so, the idea of standing face to face with the same creatures whose shipmates I had killed aboard their vessel only two days previously made me wish I was wearing rubber underpants and bicycle clips.

Beside me, Anne finished leafing through the briefing papers and handed them back to me. Before I could take them, though, Smythe snatched them and stuffed the top-secret documents into his inside jacket pocket.

"I'll have those, thank you very much," he said. "So, Mrs. Lewis, what did you think?"

Anne kept her gaze straight ahead, the back of the chauffeur's head in the middle of her field of vision. "I don't believe a word of it."

"I thought you might say that," I sighed.

"What's that supposed to mean?" She shot me an angry look.

"It means that I knew you wouldn't believe what it said in the papers," I replied calmly. "Now, don't take this the wrong way, Anne, but your viewpoint has been somewhat polarized by your work in the UFO field."

"That's a load of crap!" Anne retorted furiously. "I have an absolutely open mind, but what it says in those papers about the Greys being some insidious enemy is simply inconsistent with the vast majority of reports that we've received from hundreds of abductees."

I saw Smythe smiling into his hand and grew angry with myself for allowing the argument to develop. He was delirious that Anne and I disagreed about the subject of UFOs so acutely. Divide and conquer and all that garbage. I decided that I was not going to give him the satisfaction of seeing my ex-wife and I on opposite sides of the fence. "You're right, Anne," I said after pretending to consider the issue for a few moments. "There is a lot of evidence to refute the claims in those documents." I turned my gaze to Sir Donald. The smile had vanished from his chiselled face. "How do you explain that, boss?"

"I don't have to explain anything to you," he responded, obviously irked by my change of tack. "But I can assure you that every word in those documents is absolutely true. They were drawn up for the NATO joint chiefs and are totally accurate."

"You mean NATO knows of the supposed Grey threat?" I queried.

"Of course they do. How do you suppose we get the resources to counter the alien menace?"

I knew that he was telling the truth, but for Anne's sake, I decided to keep up my sceptical act. Out of the corner of my eye, I saw the telephone box in Cranbourne zip by and realized that we were almost there. I thought of Robert again and the guilt that had nestled in the pit of my stomach rose to the surface once more. I wanted to blame somebody for his death and at the moment, the only person I could think of was myself. True, he had been killed by a bullet fired by one of Smythe's men and it was my abduction by the Greys that had started this whole sordid adventure, but from my perspective, the entire responsibility for my friend's murder rested solely on my shoulders. When all of this was over—if ever—I would go and see Robert's parents and try to explain what had happened. If I could find the courage in my heart.

"What about the Russians?" Anne's question snapped me out of my self-pity and I regarded Smythe intently. "There have been rumours that the Soviets had recovered alien technologies. Is there any truth in that?"

"You both seem to be interrogating me," smiled the Orion head. "I hope you understand that if you are presented with the opportunity to tell any of this to the media, I will deny all knowledge and you will not be taken at all seriously."

"Personally, I don't think that either of us is going to come out of this alive," I admitted. Anne looked at me, shocked by my frankness. "I believe that as soon as my usefulness is no longer an issue, I will be killed. They are only keeping you alive to ensure my cooperation."

"Nonsense!" snorted Quentin-Smythe. "Ah, here we are."

The Rolls Royce scrunched to a halt in front the repaired main gate of the base. Smythe displayed his ID to the guard and the car was waved through. The soldier eyed Anne and me suspiciously. I wondered if he was the one who had killed Robert.

In the bright morning sunshine, I got my first clear look at the facility. If it was an airbase, then it was a very compact one. Only a few buildings were visible above ground, one of them being a small control tower beside the single short runway. Smythe explained that originally this base was assigned to a squadron of Harrier jump jets so a long runway was unnecessary. A curtain of tall pines surrounded the whole facility, looking quite odd in the middle of the vast, empty moorlands. As we approached the hangar, I saw that it was not the typical, iron structure one associates with airports. The massive sliding doors were set into a huge, grassy mound which probably made the building less visible from the air. A legacy of the Cold War no doubt. Huge, metal air vents protruded from the top of the mound, the only clue to the vast underground warren lying below. The doors opened before us and we glided inside.

The ear-splitting sound of the decontamination system echoed around us and as the buzzing faded, we were allowed to leave the car and enter the hidden depths of the Orion Committee's headquarters once more.

Smythe led us to an elevator and we stepped in beside him. He pressed the bottom button on a panel that housed about twenty and we felt the lift begin its descent. We stood awkwardly, unspeaking, as one does in elevators, and I suppressed the urge to break wind. The lift slid to a halt and its mirrored doors slid apart to reveal another lacklustre corridor with many unmarked doors set into its pallid walls.

"How many levels are there to this place?" asked Anne, genuinely intrigued.

"Twenty-five," replied Smythe proudly. "This is the lowest level—the detention area."

"Ah, I see," I commented as understanding forced its way into my addled brain. We were being taken to the imprisoned Greys. Smythe was wasting no time; he wanted the information that Tovey required as soon as possible.

We strolled the full length of the corridor and took several turns before Smythe stopped in front of one of the plain doors. How he could remember which portal was which, I never found out. He opened the door and stepped through into a small room where a single guard sat cross-legged on a wooden chair. He snapped to attention as his chief entered and saluted brusquely. I had noticed that many of the military personnel were not exactly over-awed by their civilian leader and the fact that he was the one giving the orders, and not some general, chagrined them somewhat.

"How are our guests, corporal?"

"Fine, sir. They have eaten the food provided and caused us no problems."

"Very good. Open the door, please. The lady will wait here."

"What?" said Anne. "I'm not..."

"The lady waits here, corporal."

"Yes, sir." The soldier produced a shiny, red card from his pocket and slid it across a glowing panel beside the inner door. There was an almost inaudible click and he turned the handle to allow Smythe and I access.

"Bill?"

"It's okay, Anne," I said. "I won't be long." I hoped to God that I was right.

I followed Smythe through the door and it closed behind me ominously. The illumination in the chamber was set at a dim twilight and at the back of the room, I could see five Greys sitting around a bare, metal table. They were taking occasional sips from beakers which were held in their spindly, reptilian fingers. In fact, the human quality of their movements surprised me; I had not expected to see them engaged in such basic acts.

They looked around as we approached and the expressions on their faces changed dramatically. I staggered as a mighty, psychic, "YOU" suddenly assailed me! I pulled a handkerchief from my pocket and wiped sweat from my forehead.

"Are you all right, Dr. Lewis?" asked Smythe, seemingly genuine concern in his tone.

"I think they recognize me," I wheezed.

"How is that possible?" asked the ministry man. "These Greys were in the engine room when their craft was brought down. They never even knew that you were aboard."

"They are a psychic species, Sir Donald," I explained. "What one knows, all knows."

Quentin-Smythe nodded in understanding and gestured for me to approach the quartet of aliens. I was reticent to do so—I could sense their hatred for me and it reverberated around my head like the knell of doom. But I gathered my senses and stepped towards the table.

"Hello," I said, my voice wavering slightly. "I mean you no harm..."

"You murdered our brothers. We have nothing to say to you!"

Well, at least I knew where I stood with them. "I'm sorry for what happened on board your ship, truly I am. But I was only defending myself. I had a mission to accomplish."

"You're petty, primate matters do not concern us. Our brothers will find new vessels and return to complete their work."

I could not tell which of the Greys was communicating with me. Perhaps all of them were, but that was not consistent with my abduction experience. Then, I had heard individual alien voices in my head. Suddenly, one of the creatures stood and glared at me with its huge, black eyes.

"I am speaker for these vessels here today."

"Vessels?" I asked. "Are there other ships coming?"

"What are they saying to you?" Sir Donald had stepped up beside me and was whispering in my ear.

"Remove this one from the room and we shall speak with you. His thoughts are dark, his vessel is not required here. If it does not leave, we shall not speak."

I turned to the only other human in the room. I use the term human' in the widest possible sense, of course. In my view, Smythe was no more human than these beings before me. "Er, Sir Donald, they have asked for you to leave the room."

"What?" he flapped. "I have no intention of leaving!"

"If you do not go, they say that they will not speak to me." I shrugged. "I suggest that you wait outside with Anne."

Smythe breathed heavily. "Very well. But I expect a full report when you re-emerge."

I nodded and watched as he left the chamber. When I returned my attention to the Greys, I saw that they were all seated once more. There was a spare chair at the end of the table and I took it, resting my elbows on the cold, Formica surface between the aliens and me. I sensed a snort of disgust from one of the creatures and an image of a chimpanzee with its elbows on the table flashed across my mind's eye. Interesting, I thought. They continue to retain social taboos and protocols, even though they are far more technologically advanced than us. Obviously, they see placing one's elbows on the table as the act of a primitive animal, rather like eating with your mouth open is to some of our cultures. An interesting discovery, but essentially useless in our present situation.

I knew that they could read my mind, but I decided to voice my questions audibly. I was pretty certain that there were hidden surveillance cameras and microphones everywhere around us. If Smythe and his cronies knew what questions I was asking, then they could trust that the aliens and I were engaged in relevant conversation and not just idle chitchat. Not that I would anyway—how do you chew the fat with a totally alien species to begin with? I wouldn't know.

"You referred to Sir Donald as a vessel. Did you mean his body? Do you see your own bodies as vessels?"

"Yes. The vessel holds the essence of our being. If the vessel ceases to be, then the essence returns to the One and is allocated a new vessel in the fullness of time."

"I see. We call that process reincarnation, but to many on this world it is just a myth, a story fabricated by pranksters."

"Your culture's beliefs do not interest us, but we sense that you have some grasp of the truth. That is why we are willing to speak with you and only you."

I was flabbergasted. "I don't understand. How could I even imagine what your beliefs are. We are two species separated by almost infinite volumes of time and space."

"Time and space are meaningless in the eyes of the One. All creatures are born of the One and when they die, they return to the One." The Grey spread its arms as if to encompass not just the occupants of the room, but the whole world and beyond. "We are all One. Your essence, our essence, the essence of the simplest creature on your world is the same as the essence of the One."

"You mean the universe. The One you speak of is the universe itself." My knowledge of astronomy came to the fore. "All our molecules are born in the hearts of stars and when we die, our atoms return to the hearts of stars. The universe is both infinite and finite at the same time, is that what you are saying?" The Grey nodded. "All matter in the cosmos is re-used, nothing is wasted and nothing is destroyed. We are made of the same stuff, just in differing arrangements."

The creature's thin mouth curved upwards slightly and I was almost overcome by the wave of compassion that flooded into my mind. But behind that shared feeling of tenderness, I could sense something else, the love of a proud parent tempered by the sorrow over a disobedient sibling. Things were beginning to fall into place.

"Are we, humanity, are we your children?"

"In a sense. We created your species." Did I sense guilt from the creatures? "It was a great experiment. Perhaps our greatest accomplishment and maybe our greatest mistake. When our race had reached a level where we could understand the intricacies of the One, we thought that we could emulate Its power to a certain degree. As the One breathed life into our species, we strove to breathe existence into a species of our own design. It is easier to show you how we fell from grace with the One."

I snapped back in the chair as images crashed into my mind. I saw a vast fleet of triangular spacecraft gliding towards a small, blue-green sphere. Earth. This was their planet. Not their homeworld, but simply a part of space that fell under their control. The ships slid effortlessly through the thick atmosphere, their perfectly designed hulls negating the friction that tries so hard to render our own primitive space capsules into lumps of smouldering metal.

The ships sped over vast forests and plains before silently and instantaneously coming to a halt over a particular semi-forested area. Far below, dozens of screeching, ape-like creatures fell to their knees as if in supplication to the sleek, black starships. Then they were enveloped in the all too familiar light and I knew that they had been transported into the one of the UFOs. The next sequence of images flipped by so rapidly that I was of the impression that the Greys did not want me to see too much of the next stage of their experiment. I got impressions of vast labs and storage chambers. Endless row upon row of containers holding body parts and immensely powerful computers storing genetic data. Massive clear vats of bubbling, green fluids appeared, each tank possessing the form of a hominid, each one more advanced than the last.

The final image I was shown was that of a gargantuan operation of releasing the fully developed human species into the wild.

"We monitored the development of our children for several thousand of your years and when we were content that they were not in danger of dying out, we left, happy in the knowledge that they were a part of the One, as we were."

"What went wrong?" I asked. I knew that Smythe wanted me to get information about the workings of their spacecraft, but felt that this was infinitely more important. "Why did you consider our genetic creation to be your greatest failing?"

The creature appeared to sigh, as though this entire conversation was an act of contrition and that he alone was confessing the sins of his race and asking for divine forgiveness.

"The One is perfection. The One is infinitely wise. The One does not create species without cause, as we had done with yours. The One took vengeance on us."

I did not understand what the Grey was trying to say. The universe is not a living organism, it is not sentient. I explained my concerns.

"Not only is the One aware, It is quick to punish those that attempt to imitate Its powers." The alien looked to its partners and they nodded slowly, lowering their large heads and gazing sorrowfully into their beakers.

"What's the matter?" I asked, wondering if the conversation had come to an end.

The Grey raised its head and took a sip from its cup, leaving a ring of dampness around its lipless mouth. "After we had left your world and returned to our home, unknown to us one of our scientists had contracted a virus from one of the proto-human specimens. Unfortunately, his symptoms did not rise to the surface until he was back amongst our population."

I shook my head, feeling genuine emotion for these beings. Perhaps Anne was correct after all. Could these aliens need our help? Our pity? "A plague?" I suggested. "How many died?"

"You misunderstand, human. It was no plague virus that we brought home but something far more dangerous and lethal. The virus that the scientist had contracted was a genetic creation of our own design. It was created and added to your genome to foster your procreation. We had to be certain that your species did not die out, so we inserted the virus into your genetic cells to make your race permanently fertile."

Of course, I thought. Most animals on Earth only mate during certain seasons of the year. Man is one of the few large creatures that can mate all year round. So it was no accident that the human population of Earth had risen exponentially since its appearance. We were genetically imbued with the desire to procreate all the time. I wondered why we enjoyed it so much, when to other animals it seemed more of a chore!

"What did the virus do to your race, then?"

"Over the following generations, the virus spread through our populace and our numbers grew rapidly. The cause of the dramatic population growth was not discovered until recently, so we returned to your world and began a program to obtain a cure."

"It's that bad back home?" I enquired. I couldn't believe that a race with such far-reaching technical knowledge could allow its numbers to grow to such a point where drastic steps were required to be taken. "Couldn't you do anything to slow or halt your population growth?"

"Our affinity with the One does not allow the use of birth control. The One created us, so Its laws must be obeyed."

"But you broke that law when you created us," I countered. "You should accept responsibility for your actions. You can't just begin your experiments on us again. We are your responsibility."

"That is correct. You are our responsibility. That is why we must purge the One of your race and redeem ourselves in the eyes of the One."

I jumped from my chair, sending it crashing to the floor. “What? Purge us? We’re not cattle you know, we are sentient beings not some bug that needs...”

“You are our creation! This is our world! We shall do as we please and as the One demands!”

The Grey was beginning to sound like some extreme sort of religious zealot. Anne would have kittens when she heard about this. They were not here just to study us. Their real goal was to find a cure for the virus they had created and then erase us from the planet they claimed as their own. The Greys had played God and it had backfired on them. Now they wanted to repent and the only way that they could do that was to extinguish six billion human lives.

The Grey obviously read my emotions because it stood to face me and said, “Our honesty has shocked you? We sensed that you understood our goals. That you appreciated the magnitude of our failing against the One. A cloud has fallen over your mind. A dark and terrible cloud, much like the one who leads this group of humans here. Your heart has become dark, we will no longer speak with you.”

The alien sat back down and I sensed them retreat from my mind, like a dream fading in the morning. I set my chair back onto its legs and walked quietly away from the table. I raised my hand to knock on the locked door, but then said, “We will not allow you to destroy us. We will fight you if necessary.”

“Your kind shall not succeed. The One will prevail,” came the whispering reply.

I rapped on the door and it opened immediately. I stepped out of the room into the brightly lit antechamber. Anne and Smythe were pacing furiously, the guard standing stiffly beside the door.

"Well?" demanded Sir Donald. "Did you learn anything?"

"I learned something all right, but not what you might have expected. We need to talk and my plan of sticking a gun to their heads may be our only method of extracting information from them."

CHAPTER SIXTEEN

To my surprise, Quentin-Smythe gave me an hour to collect my thoughts and make some notes for my debriefing. It was almost lunchtime and I was famished so I asked Anne to join me in the base's large cafeteria. I had made a decision and required her guidance as to whether it was the correct course of action to take.

We found a deserted table in the centre of the brilliantly lit room and while Anne sat herself down, I made my way to the self-service counter and helped myself to two mugs of coffee. On my return, I ensured that nobody on the neighbouring tables was paying any attention to our presence. Handing Anne her drink, I sat down opposite and regarded her intently. She took a sip of the foul government brew and set the mug onto the tabletop.

"What's on your mind, Bill?" she asked. "I know that look. You're plotting something."

"The Greys, your friends, they told me something and I don't know whether or not to let Smythe and his cronies in on it."

She glanced around, obviously performing the same kind of reconnaissance that I had moments before. “I thought you were pretty thick with Smythe now. What could they possibly tell you that would scare you so much?”

“I’m not scared,” I retorted.

“Then why is your coffee in danger of leaping out of the cup?”

I set the mug down, realizing that Anne was correct. I had been trembling quite violently. Well, come on, I was the only person on Earth that knew of the aliens’ real intent. Wouldn’t that make you fill your knickers? I took a deep breath and a swig of coffee, which to my surprise calmed my nerves a bit. The NAAFI must put something in it for the troops.

“The Greys’ mission here is to eventually wipe out all human life on this planet.” There, I had said it. An aeon passed as Anne stared at me. I could almost hear several stars condensing out of the interstellar ether and igniting their nuclear cores. “Well?”

“You’re crazy!” she blurted. “Have you been hanging around with Wally Hopgood?”

Hopgood was an alien abduction expert who insisted that the reason for the sinister kidnappings was so that the Greys could find our weaknesses as a prelude to invasion. His theories were generally regarded as being on the loony fringe of ufology, but he had nevertheless amassed a huge following through his books and frequent convention appearances.

“No, I’ve never even met the man...”

“I have.”

We both started at the sudden, unexpected addition to our conversation. Looking up, we saw a tall, well-built man smiling down at us. He was wearing an incredibly black suit and an equally incredibly white shirt, dissected by a thin, black tie. He had close-cropped black hair and beneath that was the most unlined face I have ever seen. If he wasn't six foot plus and built like Hulk Hogan, I could have sworn that he was about twelve years old!

He shoved his open palm under my nose. "Major Ernest Armstrong, Majestic Twelve."

I shook his hand slowly, unbalanced by his casual demeanour. After introducing Anne, he invited himself to sit with us and took out a pack of cigarettes. He offered one to me and I accepted gratefully, Anne refused gracefully. Armstrong lit up and puffed for a few seconds, not saying a word, merely observing Anne and I with more than casual interest, I suspected.

"So," I piped up eventually, "Armstrong. Is that as in Neil Armstrong?"

He smiled genuinely. "No, Doctor Lewis. He is no relation, but he was my inspiration as a child." He spoke with that thick American accent that only their military can seem to pull off. Power speech, as my dad used to call it. He had done National Service, so knew all about the power of an officer's voice. If they gave you an order, you had to obey it, no matter what.

"Major, why were you earwigging our conversation?"

"Earwigging? I'm afraid that I don't know that expression, Mrs. Lewis."

"Eavesdropping," I chipped in.

"Ah, eavesdropping." He smiled again, blue smoking pouring from each nostril like the space shuttle's booster rockets. "Earwigging, I like that. It's my job, Mrs. Lewis, and I only caught the final part of your chat about Mr. Hopgood. He is a good man, if a little paranoid. I met him once at a conference in New Mexico. Of course he didn't realize that I was with Majestic. Shame really."

"What is?" I asked curiously.

"That he was so close to the truth about our spindly little friends."

I looked across at Anne. She shrugged, obviously unimpressed by this genial Yank. "So close to the truth?" I prodded.

"Doctor, we know all about your conversation with the Greys. Majestic telepaths were monitoring the conversation." He stubbed out his cigarette in the ashtray on the table. "Our governments have known about their agenda for several years. It's one of the main reasons why we haven't notified the public. Can you imagine the global panic if we admitted that aliens were trying to wipe us out?"

"I don't believe it," said Anne quietly. "How can a race so advanced be driven by such base emotions?"

"I suggest you listen carefully to your husband's statement at the debriefing." Armstrong turned his gaze towards me. "You are going to tell Smythe everything, aren't you?"

"I suppose so." Like I said, power speech.

"In that case, I believe that the briefing room is ready. If you'll both follow me."

He stood up and, like automatons, we followed suit. We left the cafeteria and headed for one of the installation's many briefing rooms. The major held open the door for us and we entered, noticing that Smythe, Tovey and several military brass were already present.

Smythe crossed the room and held out his hand to Armstrong. "Major, so good to see you again." Old buddies, I surmised. "I didn't expect your team here so soon."

"Well, when we got Doctor Tovey's message, we caught the first Super-Valkyrie over here." He smiled over at Graeme. "Doctor? My team is waiting for you."

Tovey scurried out of the room and Armstrong closed and locked the door behind him. He ushered us to two of a dozen seats that were arranged around a large conference table. The military bigwigs eyed us suspiciously and I did my best to avoid eye contact with any of them. I did notice that not one of them was less than a two-star general and the majority were American. Smythe seated himself at the head of the table, the king fish in this particularly murky pond, and shuffled a stack of papers on the table. Armstrong returned to the door and stood with his hands crossed in front of him. Good dog, I thought.

"Now then, Doctor Lewis," said Smythe after a lengthy pause. "If you would be so good as to tell us what you learned from our guests."

I cleared my throat and nervously told the table (literally, I told the table) what I had managed to extract from the Greys. When I had finished, the officers muttered amongst themselves and I caught the occasional, "useless", "common knowledge" and "waste of time" from them. I figured that I hadn't discovered anything new for them to chew on and they were obviously disappointed.

One of the generals leaned forward on his elbows. "Doctor, how come you didn't ask them about their ship? Your orders were to extract information relevant to the reactivation of their vessel."

"I'm sorry, general," I replied quietly. "But the conversation did not have time to get around to that topic." A surge of anger rushed from the pit of my stomach. "And, if I might add, the fact that I was not informed of your group's previous intelligence probably contributed to my failure to draw any useful information from the Greys."

"What do you mean?" asked another knob.

"When they told me of their intentions, I was obviously horrified. I think they sensed my horror and refused to answer any more questions." I pointed at the papers in front of each of them. "If your psychics are that good, then why isn't it in those reports or whatever they are."

"Look, Lewis, your orders were..."

"Gentlemen, please," interjected Smythe. "Now, Doctor Lewis is right. We should have briefed him more thoroughly before sending him in. That way he would have been more prepared for the truth. I accept full responsibility. However, the timely arrival of Major Armstrong's team makes this conversation moot." His eyes scanned everybody around the table. "Our next decision is simple: What do we do with the aliens in our possession?"

"Eliminate them." This came from one of the Americans, a four-star general. "In fifty years, we have never been able to keep one of them alive for more than a few weeks at any rate. Better to put them out of our misery." A chuckle rippled around the table.

"What are you animals saying?" Anne had shot to her feet. "You can't just kill them. They are intelligent beings not cattle."

"The fact is, miss, that they see us as the cattle. Do you have any idea how many of our people they kill each year?"

"No, but..."

"Three and a half million." Anne's jaw bounced off the tabletop and returned with such force it rattled her teeth. "And those are conservative estimates. The Joes you see on TV telling us that they've been abducted by aliens are the lucky ones. Most don't come back! This year alone we've lost four armoured divisions to them."

"What?" I cried, incredulous.

"Didn't you know that this was a shooting war?" asked one of the British officers.

"Not on this scale," I replied honestly. "How do you keep a war like this secret?"

"We don't," said the four-star general. "Why do you think there are American and British troops stationed all over the world fighting other countries' battles? Half of them are fighting much more dangerous enemies."

I was overwhelmed by the sudden enormity of the situation. I had convinced myself that I was dealing with a small, covert group dedicated to keeping the public out of a private little conflict with a mostly harmless race of aliens. Now, as I observed the stern faces in front of me, I realized that the Greys were a major threat to us. Not only were they experimenting on the human race, they were in more or less open conflict with us. I watched Anne slide back into her seat, the look on her face betraying her own inner struggle. All of her life she had believed that the Greys were a benevolent species merely observing us without too much interaction. Now the truth had been rammed into her mind that they were the greatest enemy the world has ever known. I could tell that she found it difficult to imagine these slight, silent beings as the nemesis of every human on Earth, but I had personally experienced how savage the Greys were capable of being. I still bore the scars and bruises left by their physical assault on me during my incursion aboard their vessel.

The Greys may have been a spiritual, God-fearing race, but that did not exclude them from committing terrible acts of aggression. The Conquistadors had claimed that they were doing God's work when they destroyed the Incas. However, the general's callous attitude towards the Greys made my stomach perform backflips.

Executing the captive aliens would be pure murder, in my opinion. At that moment I didn't care that we were at war, albeit an undeclared one, I could not allow five intelligent beings to be killed in cold blood. If galactic historians were watching these events unfold, I would not allow the human race to be viewed as mindless savages, destroying anything that was feared or not understood. I had to find a way to save the lives of the creatures without any loss of life on either side. Unfortunately, I had no idea how to pull off such an impossible feat.

I was still deep in thought when Anne nudged me with her elbow. The generals were filing out of the room, leaving us alone with Smythe and Major Armstrong. Sir Donald's eyes were fixed on me. I could feel my subatomic structure altering by the sheer force of that stare.

"I hope that you are not considering doing something silly," he said after the room had been cleared of military paranoiacs. "I've seen that look on your face before."

"I'm not sure what you mean, Sir Donald."

"Doctor Lewis, twice already you have launched yourself and others into reckless and, on both occasions, lethal paths. I sincerely hope that you are not plotting something in a similar vein."

"Of course not. I'm not stupid, you know." Smythe's comments stirred up memories of Robert and Lieutenant Reese, both killed as I tried to expose Orion's duplicity. The gaunt man was correct—I was personally responsible for the deaths of two fine men. The fact that I had not squeezed the triggers was irrelevant. If I had not been so obsessed with exposing Orion, those two men would be alive today. I wondered what Robert's parents were going through. And Reese's wife and children. I had called Smythe and his group murderers, but was I any different? Without considering the consequences of my actions I had led people close to me into extreme danger. I would not allow that to happen again.

But I had to find a way to save the lives of the Greys!

"I'm glad that you understand," said Smythe. "Now, all we have to do is wait until Tovey gets the ship going."

"What about Anne and me?" I asked. "You have no need for us now. What are your plans for us? Once the Greys are executed, I will be of no use to you."

"Let's not jump the gun, Doctor." He steepled his fingers in front of his face. "I think it would be best if you and Mrs. Lewis remained in your rooms for the time being."

"Will we ever be allowed to return home?" asked Anne nervously.

"Like I said, let's not jump the gun."

Armstrong held the door open for us and as we entered the corridor closed and locked the door, leaving himself alone with Smythe in the briefing room. I wondered if they were concocting a humane death for the aliens. I suddenly felt ashamed to be a part of the human race. We may have been the product of a genetic experiment gone awry, but we had clawed our way up from the proverbial gutter without any outside influences and were now spreading our influence into space. In spite of all this, we were still the fearful tribesmen, terrified of anything that might come lurching out of the forest.

On our way to our quarters, I whispered to Anne my fears for the safety of the Greys. She concurred that they should be rescued, but was surprised at my sudden defection from Smythe's camp.

"I've never been in Smythe's camp," I hissed. "After Robert and Reese, I've been trying to buy us some time. I need to know that Robert didn't die for nothing. Saving the lives of our enemies will prove not only to myself, but maybe to the Greys, that humanity may be worth saving in return."

"I hope you're right, Bill."

"So do I, love. So do I."

CHAPTER SEVENTEEN

We spent the next four days pacing around our rooms. Whenever we tried the door, it was securely locked. Smythe never called to see us, the phone never rang. Food was handed to us at regular intervals, but the stone-faced military policeman that delivered it entertained no notions of conversation, no matter how hard I tried. More than once I tried to rekindle the spark of love between Anne and I, but I figured that our situation did little to nurture any loving sentiments from either of us. I had the distinct impression that I was going stir crazy. To Anne's disgust, the MP kept me stocked up with cigarettes, so the room was constantly filled with a toxic blue haze.

"How long do you think they can keep us here?" asked Anne as we finished one of our takeaways. "Mum and dad must be going out of their minds. I used to call them once a week without fail."

"Who's to know what Orion has told them. We may even be dead as far as the outside world is concerned."

The door opened behind us and we expected to see our grim delivery boy. To our surprise, Smythe stood in the doorway, a sullen look on his grey face. It flashed across my mind that perhaps the aliens had used more of their DNA in this man than they had in the rest of us. He crossed the room and slumped down into one of the comfy chairs, his dejected air cutting a swathe through the smoky atmosphere.

"Problems?" I asked innocently.

"You could say that, Doctor Lewis." He rubbed his face with his hands and coughed lightly. "I am trying to quit cigarettes, I do wish you wouldn't smoke so much."

"Nothing much else to do when your serving time," I quipped.

"Well then, you'll be glad to hear that we have need of your services again," he replied coolly. "Tovey and his friends have been unable to reactivate the alien vessel. They have taken it apart and put it back together, but can find no way to get it going. It seems that there is no direct wiring that they can discover. A most perplexing puzzle."

"What can I hope to do to help?"

"You can speak with the Greys again."

"Sir Donald, our last conversation ended on a pretty sour note. I don't think they'll talk to me again."

"You can try, can't you?"

"Sure."

Smythe wanted to leave Anne in the apartment, but I insisted that she accompany us. As we walked through the endless corridors, she took hold of my hand and squeezed it gently to let me know that she appreciated my presence. I reciprocated.

We took the elevator to the lowest level and Smythe led us to one of the base's myriad unmarked doors. It was a different door to the one that we had used when I had spoken with the Greys the previous week. I voiced my observations to Sir Donald.

"We've had them moved," he replied simply. "You'll see why."

He opened the door and stepped through. We followed apprehensively. Before us was another door and to the side a large window looked onto a small interrogation chamber. The Greys were sat around the only table in the cell, their matchstick limbs moving gracefully as they communicated with each other. Again, I found it difficult to believe that these fluid creatures were the enemy.

On our side of the glass were three plastic chairs. One of them was occupied by an eerie-looking man in one of Majestic's black suits. He stood as we approached and held out his hand.

"Doctor Lewis, Mrs. Lewis, this is Mr. Quaid, one of Majestic Twelve's top telepaths."

Pleased to meet you, I thought while shaking his hand.

"Likewise," replied the American with a voice that chilled my very soul.

Smythe grinned (not a pleasant sight) and gestured for Anne to sit down. "When you go in, Doctor Lewis, Mr. Quaid will monitor your conversation."

"Don't you trust me?" I asked.

"Frankly, no," said Smythe honestly. "But we trust the aliens even less." He sat down beside Anne and looked up at me. "In you go, then."

"Break a leg," said Anne, smiling encouragement.

I opened the inner door and stepped into the dimly-lit cell. The Greys turned to face me as I entered. I suddenly felt nauseous and had to grip the doorjamb as a wave if dizziness swept over me.

We shall have no intercourse with you.

"I'm glad to hear that," I stammered as I swallowed a mouthful of bile. "None of you are my type."

Your heart is not of the One. We have nothing to say to you.

"Look, kids," I said, cautiously stepping towards the table. "I have to talk to you. You have to tell me how to start your ship again. If you don't cooperate, these men will kill all of you." I pointed to the window and saw that it was mirrored on this side.

We will not discuss anything with a creature as primitive as you. But there is one subject we are prepared to speak with. An image of Anne appeared in my mind's eye. She is beyond the glass. We shall talk with her and her alone.

I looked at my reflection in the two-way glass and shrugged. I left the Greys and stepped back into the observation room. Anne looked terrified. I assumed that the telepath had been doing a running commentary of my conversation, speaking the alien's voices out loud.

"Bill, I can't go in there," she trembled.

I squatted down in front of her and took her hands in mine. "It'll be all right. They can't hurt you. Just go in, ask the questions and come back out. If they like you, they'll talk to you."

"Please, Mrs. Lewis." Smythe was staring at Anne with puppy dog eyes (again, not a pretty sight). "You must try."

She stood up and dried her sweaty palms on the legs of her jeans. I looked to Quaid. He was concentrating on the aliens in the other room. I gave Anne a hug and whispered in her ear, "Remember what we discussed the other day." She nodded and walked through the door.

I watched her approach the aliens and sit down in the only vacant chair. The Greys were regarding her intently, their huge eyes glistening slightly in the diffuse light. Anne's quivering voice crackled through a speaker above the window.

"Hello," she said. "You said that you would talk to me."

"They're blocking me!" exclaimed Quaid. "I can't hear them." He began trying to force his way through their mental barricade and sweat began to bead his forehead. Finally, he banged his fists against his thighs. "Dammit, I can't get through."

"It's quite all right, Mr. Quaid," consoled Smythe. "I'm sure that Anne will tell us all that we need." It was the first time I had heard him refer to Anne by her first name. "Let's just listen, shall we?"

It was a strange experience, listening to one side of a conversation, but we could grasp the gist of the discussion.

"I need to ask you some questions," we heard her say.

"Yes I am afraid."

"Well, I've never met an extra-terrestrial before." I saw one of the Greys smile.

"The One? I'm not sure I understand."

"Oh, I see. Yes you could say that. I like to believe that anything is possible."

"Get to the point, Anne," said Smythe impatiently.

"She's doing her best," I spat. "Give her a chance for crying out loud."

"I have to ask you how to power up your ship." The Greys looked to one another.

"I see. I'll try. Yes, he is a good man. I think you just frightened him, that's all."

One of the Greys looked directly at me. I knew that it couldn't see me through the mirrored glass, but I smiled at it nevertheless. It smiled back.

"Is that it? And that's the only way it can be reactivated? Okay, I'll tell them." Anne stood up and turned towards the door. "Thank you for speaking with me. I hope the One blesses you too."

When she rejoined us in the observation room, I was amazed by the look on her face. It was almost glowing, as though she had conversed with God himself. I was reminded of my Sunday school classes when the teacher had described Moses after he came down from Mount Sinai. The Bible states that his face glowed after speaking with Jehovah. Could Moses have been contacted by the Greys? I could imagine the ancient astronaut' exponents drooling all over the floor if they had been here with us. I stood and allowed Anne to sit down. She was smiling serenely.

"Well?" said Smythe succinctly. "Did they tell you anything? I got the impression that they did."

"Oh yes," she replied. "They told me how to restart the ship. Unfortunately for you, it can only be restarted by one of them with a telepathic signal."

"Typical!" yelled the government man. He turned his attention to Quaid. "I don't suppose you could do anything?"

"Sorry, sir. The aliens are still blocking me. Without the specific telepathic instructions, it will be impossible for us to get the vessel up and running."

Smythe glared at Anne. "Did they tell you the code?"

"Sorry, Sir Donald, it has to be one of them. The ship would know of any alien mind that attempted to interact with it."

"What do you mean, the ship would know'?" I asked. "Is it alive?"

"Not exactly, but it does use organic circuitry in its computer network that act as a highly advanced form of artificial intelligence. Any telepathic message that does not match the neural patterns of the Greys is ignored. This prevents their ships falling into enemy hands. Any back engineering would result in only minor advances in more primitive cultures."

Smythe ran his fingers through his hair. "Well, I suppose that is that. I have no choice but to use more threatening methods of extracting information from them. It looks like you were correct after all, Doctor Lewis. We may have to hold a gun to their heads to get any cooperation from them."

"Sir Donald," Anne interrupted, "the Greys will reactivate the ship for you."

"What? Why?"

"Because they do not wish to die. Simple as that. Their survival instincts are very powerful. If giving you access to their technology is the only way to save their lives, then they will give you what you want." Anne glanced at me and winked imperceptibly. "But they say that Bill and I must be present when they power up the ship."

"That is their only demand?" Smythe was flummoxed.

Anne nodded. I suggested that we return to our rooms while Smythe consulted with the other members of Orion and Majestic. He agreed and dismissed us with a wave of his hand.

Once back in our rooms, Anne told me exactly what the Greys had told her. Before she started, I warned her that Smythe probably had the suite bugged.

"He doesn't."

"How can you be so sure?" I enquired.

"The Greys told me. While I was speaking out loud to them, we were having a whole different conversation inside our heads. That was why they were blocking Quaid. Bill, they want to go home."

"Who doesn't?" I blurted. "But I don't see how we can help. Smythe will have dozens of armed guards around those things when they reactivate the ship."

"The guards will not be a problem," she smiled knowingly and told me of the plan.

Once their vessel had been reactivated, they Greys would dispose of the troops on board (I didn't dwell for too long on that part of the plan) and send a signal to their nearest outpost (she didn't expound on where this might be). Within minutes, a ship would be sent for them. The deal was that if we helped them escape, they would allow us to use the ship to publicize the alien presence on Earth.

The Greys intended to literally land on the Whitehouse lawn. Once there it will deposit Anne and me and take off again, performing a series of impossible aerobatic manoeuvres, for the benefit of the watching world, before departing.

I asked why a second ship was required if they intended to use the first one to evade capture. Anne said that the Greys leave very little to chance. They are aware that we can bring their ships down. The summoning of a second spacecraft was merely a precautionary measure in case anything might happen to the first.

"How come they trust you so much?" I asked her.

"They said that of all the humans they had encountered, my heart was the closest to the One. My inquisitive, searching mind encapsulated the very essence of what it means to be sentient."

"But I'm a scientist, you can't get more inquisitive or searching than that," I said, quite a bit put out that the Greys did not consider me as sentient.

"That's half the problem with humans. We put too much stock in science. We feel that science offers all the answers when it clearly does not."

"You're beginning to sound like one of those loony UFO cults!" I exclaimed.

"I'm only telling you what they told me, Bill," she said calmly. A bit too calmly, if you ask me. Ever since her chat with the aliens, Anne acted as though she had had a spiritual revelation. I voiced my concerns.

"Don't worry, Bill, it's still me in here. I'm not about to proclaim myself as the Second Coming. But when you're told that you are the most perfect human specimen on the planet, it kind of boosts your ego!"

"I still prefer Cindy Crawford, if you ask me," I muttered. "Go on then, what else did they reveal to your perfect mind?"

"That was it basically. If everybody on earth develops like me, then the human race might stand a chance. Unfortunately for us, the faulty gene the Greys inherited from us has sealed our doom as far as they are concerned."

"So they still intend to wipe us out?" I observed.

"Looks like it. Unless we can find a way to bring them round."

At that moment, Smythe and Tovey entered the room and told us to follow them. They were going to let the aliens restart the ship. Tovey was rocking on his heels like an excited schoolboy on Christmas morning. He thought he was going to receive the greatest toy in the universe. I couldn't wait to see his face when the Greys turned out to be Indian givers!

CHAPTER EIGHTEEN

As we entered the hangar, my jaw dropped. This was the largest room that I had ever seen, dwarfing the biggest conference centres I had lectured in. Hovering in the centre of this vast space, the Greys' ship was surrounded by dozens of armed troops. Brilliant floodlights washed the area with dazzling radiance, yet the black, polyhedral form absorbed every photon that struck its immense hull. A huge, triangular black hole created by a technology thousands of years in advance of our own.

"Good grief," whispered Anne, awestruck by the sight. She tapped Tovey on the shoulder. "I thought it was powered down. How come it's hovering?"

"The design of the hull appears to incorporate some kind of anti-gravitational material."

Anne looked to me and shrugged her shoulders. "That sounds a bit vague, Graeme," I observed. "What kind of material?"

"Spectroscopic readings have detected a steady stream of inverse gravitons emanating from every square inch of the craft," explained Anne's old flame.

"If I recall my particle physics classes," I said. "Gravitons can only be detected in the largest particle accelerators."

"Usually, but we are dealing with a technology on a whole different level." The scientist rubbed his beard with five stubby fingers. "I think that many of the ship's systems operate using technology that utilizes quantum mechanics."

"You think?" I persisted. "It sounds to me like you're in over your head."

"Look, Lewis..."

Major Armstrong arrived right on cue and interrupted what might have been a very agreeable argument. I had been itching to get my hands on Tovey (in a theoretical sense, of course), but I would have to wait, Dolph Lundgren was waiting to take our group aboard the ship.

He led us to a set of aeroplane boarding stairs and ushered us up to what appeared to be some kind of opening in the side of the vessel. The portal's design was unlike anything I had ever seen. It seemed as though a huge zip fastener had been opened and the hull of the ship pulled apart to form an almost organic-looking entrance.

I looked down from the top of the stairs, the guards below remained motionless, their weapons slung but, I guessed, ready to be used at a moment's notice. Then I walked into the ship.

It took me a few seconds to catch up with Anne and the others. They were making their way through dark, damp corridors with Armstrong leading the way. A few paces ahead, I saw Tovey rubbing his hands together nervously. It was evident that his career with the Orion Committee hung on what the Greys did with their unbelievable vessel. To be completely honest, after what Anne and I had been through, I hoped that he ended up working at some research facility in, say, Antarctica. If what we had in mind actually succeeded, that possibility may actually occur. I couldn't wait!

Armstrong stopped in front of a blank wall. I knew from my previous excursion aboard this very ship, that we were on one side of a door. The Majestic man stepped through, his body melting into and then disappearing through the solid liquid. Smythe and Tovey followed suit, but Anne hesitated, apprehensive. I took her hand and spoke soft words of encouragement. Then we stepped through together.

I was expecting a huge chamber with flashing lights and glowing conduits, something akin to the engine room of the U.S.S. Enterprise in Star Trek. I was bitterly disappointed.

The room was small, only about twenty feet square, with a ceiling barely seven feet above our heads. In the centre of the chamber stood a small tree trunk shaped structure and around this were placed three panels, of which only one appeared to be in operation. In front of its smooth surface, strange, unearthly hieroglyphs were projected into thin air. These symbols changed constantly, as though it were some alien computer program in operation. Nearby, surrounded by half a dozen soldiers in full battle dress, stood the five surviving Greys, and to one side was Mr. Quaid, the Majestic telepath.

Tovey stepped across to the working console and turned to face us.

"As I said earlier, Sir Donald, this is the only working piece of equipment on board. It appears to be a back up system of some kind and is baffling to both myself and the team of Majestic philologists.

"Those symbols almost look Egyptian," I chipped in. Anne concurred.

Tovey nodded his head. "Yes, almost Egyptian, but different enough to be totally incomprehensible."

"They are scripted thought forms," said Anne abruptly. We all looked to her, intrigued by her sudden insight. "The Greys just told me," she explained.

"Mr. Quaid?" said Smythe, raising his voice slightly.

"Sorry, sir. They are still blocking me. No matter how hard I try, I keep getting confused images."

"Keep trying," ordered Armstrong. The telepath nodded and focused once more on the aliens.

"Sir, I think we should let the Greys do their stuff," said the major, stabbing his thumb towards the silent quintet. Smythe nodded and Armstrong walked across to the aliens. "Okay fellas, it's all yours."

"Mrs. Lewis, if they contact you again, I expect you to inform us immediately." Smythe glared at Anne as though she were one of his lowest underlings.

"Of course," she lied. "They are starting the ship...now."

Within a fraction of a second, the two dark panels flickered into life and a resonant hum echoed around the chamber. I heard several surprised gasps, then a bright, warm flash seared my retinas. When I opened my eyes again, I saw that Smythe, Armstrong and the troops had vanished. Only me, Anne and Tovey remained in the engine room with the Greys.

I ran towards the nearest alien. "What happened? Where are they?"

Follow me and I will show you. The creature gracefully slid past me and out of the room. I told Anne and Tovey to follow me and headed after the speedy alien. We found it waiting for us outside the control room portal. It squelched through the wall, with us a step behind, and glided towards one of the many consoles at the front of the area. Its reptilian fingers danced across the panel and the walls shimmered into an image of the hangar outside.

The troops now had their weapons trained on the ship, but were holding fire for the time being. Behind them, arguing furiously were Smythe and Armstrong. From the manner of their gesticulations, I could tell that the American wanted the soldiers to fire on the ship, but Smythe obviously didn't want his prize damaged any further. To one side I could just make out the aircraft boarding steps. They had somehow been overturned and were lying on concrete floor, useless.

We must leave now. Prepare yourselves.

As I watched, the image of the hangar distorted and I could see several of the soldiers drop their weapons in horror. Then, like water running down a plughole, the image rotated and stretched, finally returning to normal as an image of the night sky. I looked down, expecting to see the base below us. My knees buckled as I saw cloud tops and beneath them land and sea. In the distance, the curve of the Earth stretched as far as I could see on either side. We were in orbit!

Something caught my eye. Several somethings, in fact. Straining my vision, I could make out half a dozen tiny shapes floating outside the spacecraft. One of them drew closer and its form became clear. I gasped and held my hand to my mouth.

The soldier's contorted body echoed the terror which had been literally frozen onto his face. It was apparent that he and the others I could see had been too close to the starship when it had activated its propulsion system and had been pulled with us into what I surmised was a wormhole. Freezing almost instantly when we emerged into orbital space, they had stood no chance of survival whatsoever. My observations were confirmed when the body of the sergeant (he was now close enough to define the stripes on his sleeve) collided with the side of the Greys' vessel. The force of the impact shattered his deep frozen body into a million pieces, each fragment entering its own orbit before finally cremating itself as Earth's gravity pulled it into a fiery embrace. The same would happen to the other bodies and I felt great pity for them and their families. How would Smythe explain those deaths? But what a way to go—five shooting stars and a brief meteor shower as your epitaph!

Tovey was transfixed by the view before him. With tears in his eyes, he sank to his knees, his mouth opening and closing wordlessly. He had not even noticed the Orion soldier's grisly demise, his raptures had been so completely enveloping. Anne had noticed and buried her face into my chest; more deaths for her conscience to deal with. If we survived this, I wondered how many hours of counselling would be required before we were truly over our nightmare experiences. Perhaps we would never recover fully.

As Anne and I held each other, I saw a portion of the Earth's surface ripple and an instant later a second triangular vessel appeared in the distance. It drew alongside our ship and came to a gentle halt a few hundred yards away, its dark shape almost indistinguishable against the sheer black of space.

At the front end of the control room, I could see that the Grey was having some difficulty operating the ship on his own. I disentangled myself from Anne's embrace and approached the busy alien.

"Need any help?" I asked, genuinely wishing to be of assistance.

No thank you. I was surprised by the creature's graciousness. I am quite able to perform my functions without assistance. It paused from its work and turned to look up at me, its huge, almond eyes reflecting starlight from above. We, my crewmates and I, apologise for our actions against your people. It gestured towards Anne and she approached tentatively. If humanity progresses as you have, becomes closer to the One, then there may be hope for your species.

"Why don't you just stop what you are doing and leave us in peace?" I asked diplomatically.

Our own survival depends on your destruction. The One demands it. On this downbeat note, the Grey returned to its work, ignoring the rest of us completely.

I turned to Anne and raised an eyebrow. "There's no news like good news."

Suddenly, the ship lurched to one side and we were all thrown across the cabin. The walls shimmered momentarily then steadied. I stared down at the blue sphere below and saw several brilliant streaks bursting out of the atmosphere and heading straight for us. Another struck home and the spacecraft shuddered again. The other craft easily outmanoeuvred the objects, but ours was being repeatedly pummelled by these weapons.

"Missiles!" yelled Anne. "Orion and Majestic are firing on us!"

"I didn't know we had anything that fast," I said.

"They're probably ion or photon driven," she explained, drawing on her knowledge of the many rumoured weapons systems that filter into UFO lore. "At a guess I'd say that they're being fired from either the Brookhaven National Laboratory in New York or from a warship in the North Atlantic. I don't understand how we keep being hit." She glanced across at the other alien vessel, which was still avoiding the lethal, hypersonic arrows. "The other ship's doing okay."

This vessel was damaged by your people's attack when we were captured, thought the Grey. I am unable to avoid your weapons.

The craft lurched again, briefly corrected its attitude and then I caught a glimpse of the ground rushing up to meet us before the walls appeared and we were tumbling blindly out of orbit.

CHAPTER NINETEEN

The natural pull of the Earth had us by the scruff of the neck and the ship's artificial gravity systems obviously had trouble coping with our reeling descent. All of us were tossed about the control room like kernels in a popcorn machine. The Grey was clinging desperately to its control station, running its fingers across the multi-coloured surface whenever the ship momentarily righted itself. Eventually, it must have keyed the correct sequence of commands and the room stopped tumbling.

Anne and I slid to the deck, breathing heavily. Then Tovey careened into me and we skidded across the polished floor and into the far wall. Graeme grunted like a bearded walrus as he unwrapped himself from me and I took great pleasure in giving him several elbow nudges in his well-padded ribs.

I pulled myself erect and staggered across to the Grey, which was frantically operating its controls. "How can you tell where we are going?" I asked, referring to the blank walls surrounding us. The creature hissed through its lipless mouth and I translated that as: "Leave me alone, I'm busy." It was the first time that I had heard the aliens utter a verbal sound. I much preferred their feathery mental dialogue to that threatening, primordial rasp.

I returned to Anne, who was dusting herself down, and pointed out a small cut on her forehead. She reached up, lightly touching the wound.

"It's nothing," she said. "What's the Grey doing?"

"Trying to land us, I think. What the hell is he doing?" I pointed to Tovey.

He was at the back of the room, attempting desperately to pass through the rear wall. It was almost comical to watch him bashing his face against the solid surface in front of him.

"I don't think it works any more," I called after watching him try a few more times. Fifteen more times to be exact.

He rubbed his forehead, where an ovoid patch of redness had formed nicely. "How are we supposed to get out?" he pleaded and began banging his fists against the wall. "LET ME OUT!" he screamed. "LET ME OUT!"

Apparently, Anne had taken about as much as she could from Tovey. She walked calmly up to him and turned him around gently, gazing lovingly into his petrified, red-rimmed eyes. Then she knocked him out with a single punch to his lower jaw. She rubbed her sore knuckles as he slid to the floor and turned to look at me.

"He was getting on my nerves," she said sweetly.

"Wow," was all I could muster.

I crossed the room and knelt down beside Tovey's inert body and checked his wrist for a pulse—just in case. He was sleeping peacefully. Which was just as well, because at that moment our entire world was turned upside down as the spacecraft hit the ground.

I felt something break as I hit the front wall of the control room and I screamed. As I slumped to the deck, I saw Anne writhing in agony a few feet to my right and Tovey came sliding along a moment later. Somehow, the Grey had escaped unscathed and was operating its controls once more. I had to give it to these creatures, they were diligent. It took a lot to put them out of commission.

I pulled myself to my feet, wincing as pain lanced throughout my abdomen, and stumbled across to Anne. She was sitting against the wall, nursing a badly scraped shin. Blood also oozed from both of her elbows. As I squatted beside her, she informed me that she was not too badly injured and told me to check on Tovey.

Fortunately for him, his unconscious state had relaxed his body enough for him to escape serious harm, but Anne's jawbreaker had swollen his chin to such a degree that he looked like he had a big, hairy pomegranate stuck to his face. I shook him and he grunted lazily. Then his eyes flickered open and he began screaming at the top of his voice, oblivious to the embolism inhabiting his lower jaw.

"Graeme, it's over." I shook him a little more violently than before and he focused on my face with tear-streaked eyes. "We're down. We're safe."

"I'm alive!" He began touching various parts of his anatomy, as if to ensure that he was still whole. "I'm alive!"

"You're alive, Graeme. Unless heaven is exactly the same as the inside of a flying saucer. Can you stand up?" He nodded and I helped him to his feet. I called across to the Grey, which was still fumbling with its switches. "Hey, Shorty, any chance of us getting out of here?"

Suddenly, we were surrounded by grass, ploughed earth, nearby trees and what appeared to be a confused crowd of several thousand people. The alien's super-focused expertise had got the walls working again. Like I said, these things were diligent.

I scanned the area, trying to ascertain where on Earth we were, when movement above caught my eye. I looked up and saw the second spacecraft hovering above us. The Grey had obviously seen it too, because it moved away from the control console and stared up at the flying triangle.

As I watched, the crowd parted and what seemed like hundreds of heavily armed troops began pushing them back, away from our stricken starship. Within minutes, a cordon had been set up about fifty yards from the crash site and the scores of onlookers had to content themselves with a no less impressive view from there. I noted that several film crews had arrived and were training their cameras on both ships. I chuckled to myself. How was Smythe going to spin his way out of this one?

More movement from above. Half a dozen huge, bristling helicopters were hovering around the second alien vessel, their weapons aimed belligerently at the mysterious intruder. I could see that the choppers had United States Air Force markings. Anne limped over to me, her eyes casting their nets over my shoulder.

"Well, I think we're in America somewhere," I said, hoping to impress with my observational skills. I indicated the numerous television cameras surrounding us. "And we'll make the Six O'clock News, if I'm not very much mistaken."

"Yep," she replied, pointing behind me with a shaking finger.

I turned round and realized exactly where we were. I felt like Charlton Heston when he sees the Statue of Liberty at the conclusion of Planet of the Apes. If Roddy McDowell came running up to me wearing a monkey suit, the illusion would have been complete.

Several hundred yards behind the crashed ship, the apex of its domed roof missing, stood the seat of American government, the Whitehouse. The remains of its shattered roof littered a trail of debris leading to the huge furrow carved by our arrival. I desperately wished that nobody had been hurt due to our impact. With this sombre thought still whirring around my addled brain, I was startled when my shoulder felt a light tap. I looked round and saw the Grey gazing up at me, the other spaceship reflecting in its immense eyes—triangular, alien pupils that have seen things no human could possibly imagine.

The time has come for me to leave.

"What about us?" I asked, not relishing the idea of being trapped inside an alien spaceship while the military decide whether or not to take pot-shots at it.

We will transport you to the outside. Prepare yourselves.

Anne looked down at the slight creature. "May the One bless you."

Your species is unlike anything our scientists envisaged. Its gaze flowed across the crowds outside and then onto the circling helicopters. Your curiosity is exceeded only by your aggression. Yet, somehow, you are growing closer to the One. If not for our own disgrace, your people would have joined us amongst the stars sooner than you could have imagined.

Anne took the being's tiny hands in hers and lowered herself to its height. "The One is forgiving. The universe rarely wastes anything—all matter has a purpose, as does all life. Perhaps our peoples could work together to find a cure for your syndrome. Our destruction would be a greater crime in the eyes of the One. Think about it."

We will.

There was a scorching flash of energy and I squeezed my eyes tight shut. When I opened them again, I saw Anne and Tovey lying on soft, green grass beside me. I also saw dozens of automatic rifles pointing at us with nervous US Marines behind them. I looked from Anne to Tovey and back again, unsure how to proceed or what to say.

Brilliant sunlight blazed down into the circle of troops and I could see that the second Grey vessel had vanished, leaving its dysfunctional twin behind, some yards to our left and almost hidden from view by numerous khaki legs. I cleared my throat.

"Take me to your leader?" I smiled.

CHAPTER TWENTY

A month later, I was sitting in Quentin-Smythe's library, sipping weak tea and exchanging pleasantries. I had broken two ribs during the crash and was still heavily bandaged and sore. Anne had escaped with cuts and bruises and Tovey's chin had receded to its usual bristled, flabby self. Both were sitting with me, listening to Smythe's resonant voice.

Within an hour of the crash, the three of us had been airlifted to Majestic Twelve's headquarters in Maryland and, after a little patchy first aid, had been thoroughly interrogated by an army of less than gentle agents. Majestic and Orion were not happy with us. Our cover story, that we had been innocent victims of the Greys' intricate escape ploy, fell on largely deaf ears. I even feared for our lives more than once. To my amazement, Tovey backed up the story and I felt a creeping respect for the ailing scientist. Over the following weeks, he seemed more like the old Graeme Tovey—the excitable UFO investigator—and less like the Orion pawn that he had been of late. It was obviously a role that he had performed under some duress. It was nice to see him finally free himself from Smythe's suffocating grasp.

A week later, we had been flown back to England. The Super-Valkyrie aircraft used for our transport was something to behold. Twice as large as Concorde and almost three times as fast with a ceiling altitude that almost took us into orbit. The plane's interior was a bit more austere, however, and we had to share our uncomfortable bench seats with a boatload of Majestic agents. There was no in-flight movie, either.

I had been correct about us making the Six O'clock News. In fact, we made all the news in every country in the world. Like it or not, our escapade had made the three of us celebrities, with our faces plastered across every bulletin and newspaper across the globe.

"3 SURVIVE FLYING SAUCER CRASH" had been one headline. "UFO TRIO STILL UNKNOWN: Survivors held at secret location" had been another. Although we had famous faces, Anne, Tovey and I were not allowed to benefit from our newfound prestige. Orion and Majestic kept us all to themselves.

The day after the crash, the president of the United States had been forced to publicly admit that the vessel had indeed been an extra-terrestrial spacecraft. His solemn, dry statement was beamed around the world. He understandably omitted any reference about the Grey's real reasons for being here, but the armed forces of every nation were placed on high alert nevertheless.

The expected riots and mass hysteria did not happen, much to everybody's amazement. The disclosure that we were no longer alone in the universe came as no surprise to a general public that had been force-fed such ideas in the last years of the twentieth century. Television and movie depictions of aliens had softened the populace up to the inevitable contact with beings from another world. Fears from the religious community, that proof of ETs would result in theological upheavals, were unfounded. Far from dissuading people of the existence of God, millions more flooded into the churches and temples of all religions. To many, it seemed that God was showing us that we were not his only children. God, the One, was truly universal and he was doing a roaring trade on Earth once more.

Of course, there were some downsides to the discovery of alien life. Memberships to extreme cults grew to record levels. Thousands were conned out of their savings, property and even their lives as many of them were brainwashed into committing suicide to be closer to the Angels Of Creation', as the Greys had become known to some.

On the whole, though, the public adjusted quickly to the revelation and life soon returned to a semblance of normality. The stock markets did not crash and the money in your pocket was worth the same as it was yesterday.

Except for me. I was broke and living on the good graces of Smythe and the Orion Committee. I had hoped that once the Greys' presence was public knowledge, I would be released and allowed to enter society once more—I had been injured in the line of duty, after all. No such luck. In fact, I was pulled even deeper into the heart of the beast that was Orion. While my personal funds amounted to less than zero, the Committee's funding actually increased after they had demanded more money to open field offices in every major city. The theory was that reported sightings of UFOs would increase dramatically in the weeks following the crash, with thc public watching the skies with ever more vigilance.

The truth was that in the month since the announcement, sightings of flying saucers had actually dropped to almost zero. This was what Smythe was telling us as we drank Earl Grey in his flamboyant home. Despite what O'Donnell had told us about his wife, I still had to clap eyes on Lady Quentin-Smythe.

"Why are you telling us this?" I was confused by Smythe's report. As far as I was concerned, the Orion Committee had no further use for either Anne or myself. Even Graeme's contributions to his employers had diminished recently. With the majority of the work on the alien ship being carried out in the States, he had relatively little to do and spent most of his time hanging around with us, much to my annoyance. I had been trying hard to get Anne's boiler going again, but Tovey acted like a bucket of cold water, dowsing our fiery passions as thoroughly as a halon extinguisher.

"I am telling you this because I believe you may have some insight about the Greys' sudden disappearance." Sir Donald sat back in the leather chair, which had replaced the more austere one we had seen the last time we had been in the ministry man's lair, and folded his arms across his chest.

"What makes you think we know anything?" Anne set down her tea on the edge of Smythe's desk.

"You and your husband were the two closest people to the aliens. Even the Majestic telepaths were unable to extract as much information out of them as you two did." He leaned forward again. "And I suspect that you were behind their escape."

“That’s ridiculous,” I replied. “We told you what happened. They were going to kidnap us for their vile experiments. If you hadn’t shot them down, we might be dead by now.”

“Why didn’t they take you with them when they escaped in the other ship?”

“I don’t know, Smythe. We’ve been through all this with Armstrong and his friends.” I lit a cigarette—a sure sign that I was getting nervous. “Look, perhaps your weapons scared them away.”

“I doubt that, Doctor Lewis. I think that they’ll come back and when they do, it will mean the end for our society.”

I blew a stream of smoke into the air. “You’re being unusually pessimistic, Sir Donald. If what you say about there being no new sightings is true, then maybe they’ve decided to leave us alone. This could be an overture to peace.”

Smythe snorted. The telephone on his desk rang, making us all jump with its shrill song. He picked it up and listened for a few seconds. “Fax a copy to my office here. No, I’ll decide when to inform the PM.” He cradled the receiver, rose from his seat and crossed to the library door. Jennings was standing silently on the other side. “Jennings, a fax is coming to my office. Would you go get it for me?” The butler nodded and ambled across the hall to one of the doors at the far side. Smythe waited patiently for the old buffer’s return. A couple of minutes later, Jennings trudged back and handed his boss some leaves of paper.

Smythe closed the door and returned to his chair, scrutinizing the sheets with a worrisome frown on his face.

The suspense was killing me and I could see that Anne and Graeme were sitting on the edges of their seats as well.

"Problem?" I enquired wistfully. Smythe ignored me and continued to scan the fax. "Well, if you don't need us any more, we'll be on our way." I stood up to leave.

"Stay." I sat down again. I was going to have to get some power speech lessons for myself.

"It's to do with the Greys, isn't it?" asked Anne.

Smythe finished his reading and slid the papers across the desk. "See for yourself."

Anne scooped them up and studied them for herself. The gamut of emotions that played across her face almost made my hair stand on end. I wasn't sure if it was good news or bad. She handed the sheets to me.

The fax contained a breakdown of data received by the Arecibo radio telescope in Puerto Rico. At over a thousand feet across, it was the largest telescope of its kind in the world. From the data, it appeared that the scientists there had received a signal of enormous power from a source somewhere within our own solar system.

The transmission was self-repeating and cycled every nineteen point four seven seconds. The bulk of the fax consisted of raw data, streams of binary digits, but a translation of the message was included on the last page.

It was a message from the Greys, cryptic and enigmatic. Anne took it to mean that peace between our peoples was imminent, that we were to benefit greatly from their permanent presence on Earth.

Smythe was less optimistic. He felt that the message was a thinly-veiled threat, intended to instil fear into us before their final invasion.

Tovey didn't know what to make of it, but I had come to expect that of him.

With the course my life had taken recently, I could not care to guess what might happen, so in some respects, I was like Graeme—aargh! I was riding those mercury rapids again, but this time, maybe I had a paddle with which to steer myself. I could be swept along as events unfolded beneath me, but now I expected the twists and turns that fate lobbed at me.

To me, the message only marked the beginning of a new adventure. An adventure that would herald in the dawn of a new age both for myself and for the whole of humanity.

The message read:

"PREPARE YOURSELVES. THE ONE AWAITS YOU."

ABOUT THE AUTHOR

Steven Johnson lives in Yorkshire, England, with his young son, Aiden. *Mercury Rapids* is his first novel.

Because it all

backfired on Them

Printed in the United States
6722

9 781592 810161